In *Confessions to a Stranger*, Danielle Grandinetti weaves a tale that is at once mysterious, suspenseful, romantic, and inspiring ... this novel is a lovely start to what is sure to be a wonderful series!

—Heidi Chiavaroli,
Carol Award-Winning Author of *The Orchard House*

Danielle Grandinetti has crafted a wonderful tale of suspense and romance that will keep you on the edge of your seat. With well-drawn characters authentic to the era, a gripping plot, and a strong message of hope, *Confessions to a Stranger* is a read I recommend!

—Misty M. Beller,
USA Today bestselling author of the Sisters of the Rockies

A Strike to the Heart is a compelling story. From the very first page, I was immersed into the thrilling action and remained gripped with intrigue until the satisfying ending. The romance escalated right along with the winding plot, creating a layered mystery that is sure to delight readers.

—Rachel Scott McDaniel,
Award-winning author of *The Mobster's Daughter*

Riveting from the first scene, *As Silent as the Night* offers a unique, edge-of-your-seat Christmas read ... A beautiful, gripping, and romantically suspenseful Christmas story you wouldn't be able to put down if you tried.

—Chautona Havig,
Author of *The Stars of New Cheltenham*

The Neighbor and the Gifts is a poignant tale that transforms a familiar carol into a stirring journey of faith, love, and danger ... For readers who love historical romance, mystery, and want a deeper meaning in their holiday stories—this one's for you.

—Natalie Walters,
bestselling and award-winning author of *Living Lies* and the *SNAP Agency* series

THE NEIGHBOR AND THE GIFTS

**Discover the Foundation
of Danielle's Bookish World**

Harbored in Crow's Nest
Confessions to a Stranger
Refuge for the Archaeologist
Escape with the Prodigal
Relying on the Enemy
Sheltered by the Doctor
Investigation of a Journalist

Bridge: His Boss's Little Sister

Unexpected Protectors
To Stand in the Breach
A Strike to the Heart
As Silent as the Night

For a complete list, visit
daniellegrandinetti.com/books

THE NEIGHBOR AND THE GIFTS

DANIELLE GRANDINETTI

Hearth Spot Press

To all those who, like me, adore Christmas
Music

In the English translation of *Noël Nouvelet*:
Sing we now of Christmas,
Noel, sing we here!

Thanks be unto God for his unspeakable gift.

2 Corinthians 9:15, KJV

CHAPTER ONE

Manitowish Waters, Wisconsin
Saturday, December 13, 1930

Olivia Larson hummed the tune to "Hark, the Herald Angels Sing" as she strode down the snow-covered main thoroughfare of her hometown—only twelve days until Christmas Morning. A wonderful thrill zipped through her. She planned to surprise Grandfather with a visit after closing the Library on Christmas Eve. The older man understood her shyness better than any—including her immediate family—ever had, so she stayed in Manitowish Waters when her parents and siblings left to follow the lumber companies west.

A pair of young boys ran down the empty street, sliding on a patch of ice before gaining traction again. She recognized them as two of her more unruly library patrons, a duo who had devoured *The Tale of Peter Rabbit* over the summer, then promptly went out to recreate some of the antics Ms. Potter described in her story. Would they enjoy *The Tale of Benjamin Bunny* just as much? Mrs. Cavenaugh had donated a monetary gift that allowed Ollie to purchase a few new books in time for Christmas. Had they arrived yet?

She glanced toward the courthouse where Mrs. Cavenaugh's husband, the judge, reigned. Snow piled high against the sides of the building, sparkling in the rare bit of sun that made its unusual appearance today. She had no doubt the clouds would return tomorrow, but for now, she would enjoy the sunlight. Evergreen boughs, all the trimmings and trappings of Christmas added a festive note to the courthouse, likely the doing of Sheriff Yarwood's new wife, the judge's former secretary. Eira Mae brought Christmas everywhere. A bit intimidating, if Ollie were honest. She could never make the library feel so ... well, Christmassy.

That inner acknowledgment lowered her guard just enough that her eyes betrayed her. Her gaze slid over to the building next to the courthouse, to the jail where Sheriff Yarwood and his deputy, the handsome Titus Wilburn, kept the peace in the county. Ollie adjusted the strap on her shoulder, the weight of the books in the bag threatening to bend her sideways. Just like thoughts of Titus always did.

No matter how she steeled herself against it, every day she walked this route to the library, her mind wandered to the deputy-that-had-been-sheriff. She'd been so proud of Titus when he took over for Sheriff Yarwood two years ago during the other man's hiatus, and she wondered how Titus felt to be demoted to deputy again. Did he feel slighted? Grateful? She wanted to ask him but didn't feel it was appropriate.

Ollie huffed. She would enjoy asking Titus a lot of things. But the truth was she'd never even managed a complete sentence around him. Ever since she and Titus were in school together, he'd always looked out for her like a big brother, and he always spared her a smile. All it did was cause a warm fuzzy feeling inside that caused every romantic story she read to fill her head. In an instant, she would dream of being a damsel in distress and how he'd rescue her. Then reality would crash in on her, and she'd stutter and stammer and run away in embarrassment.

She jerked her attention away from the jailhouse. She was over twenty years old, and if she couldn't talk to a man, she'd remain the spinster librarian her entire life. Not that she would mind. She loved encouraging children to read. If only she could flirt or, in some way, let Titus know she liked him. But no ... he'd never given her any reason to believe *he* liked *her*, at least not in *that* way.

"Hey, Ollie!" Titus's voice rang in her head. Wait, not in her imagination. His greeting was real.

She looked over in time to see him wave as he exited the courthouse, offering his usual smile. Snow crunched under his boots as he jogged across the street toward her. Her heart picked up speed, and she tucked a rogue strand of hair behind her ear. Or should she tuck it under her hat? Did she have any breakfast left on her face? Did he know she'd just been daydreaming about him? Maybe he didn't mean to talk with her. The post office was to her left. Yes, that had to be the reason he crossed the street. She'd keep on her way to the library.

But as she stepped in that direction, her heel landed on a slick bit of ice. She windmilled in an attempt to catch her balance, but the bag on her shoulder, the one filled with heavy books, dragged her backward. Her feet flew up, her head went back, and the next moment, she had landed hard on her derriere.

Titus knelt beside her, one hand supporting her back as she remained seated, the other patting her head, her shoulders, her arms. "Are you all right?" He sounded concerned. But of course he would.

"I'm fine. Stunned, but, uh, fine. Yes, fine." She refused to look at him, as if that could hide the embarrassment flooding her body with heat. Oh, the mortification. How quickly could she escape him? "I won't keep you."

"Perhaps you should visit Doc?" His fingers touched her temple, shifting the knit cap askew. "You could have broken something, bruised something. Did you hit your head?"

Ollie felt the heat rush across her face. Obviously, Titus could see her embarrassment. He'd already seen her lack of grace, what with collapsing in a heap on the ground. And she probably had snow and dirt and who-knew-what-else all across her backside. "I have to get to the library." It would be better if she could just disappear underneath the boardwalk.

"Ollie. You fell. Are you sure you aren't hurt?" He helped her stand, and her distressed-damsel-addicted heart begged to lean into his touch. Her imagination threatened to cast him as a hero slaying a dragon. Ridiculous. She reached for her bag of books, but Titus held it out of reach. "The library can wait."

Was it actually possible to spontaneously combust? Krook did in Dickens's *Bleak House*. That was fiction, but if she didn't escape Titus, she might combust too, and then she'd be splattered all over the snow-covered walk. And Titus. Gracious! She snatched her bag. "I'm fine, Ti-Titus."

"At least let me escort you." He helped her settle the bag on her shoulder.

Her cheeks had to be as red as a holly berry. Of course, a good deputy like Titus would offer to assist. What widow didn't he help? What older gentleman didn't he assist? But to be escorted by Titus because he desired her company and not out of duty? She shook her head, words trapped in her dry throat.

Titus took a step back. "As you wish."

She didn't wish, but she couldn't find the words to say otherwise. Another blast of heat shot through her at what she *did* wish, so she spun on her heel and nearly ran for the library. No, scurried like the scared little mouse she was.

Not until the library steps did she risk a glance back at where she'd left him, a block away. He'd forgotten about her already, deep in conversation as he was with Mrs. Holland, the proprietress of the Manitowish Waters Inn. If only she'd wished Titus a *Merry Christmas*. She might not get another opportunity to do so before the holiday. And it only made sense to offer the season's greeting at this time of year.

Why did he have to fluster her so she couldn't think straight?

With a sigh, she nearly stepped on the package lying on the ground before the library's large wooden door.

A brown box. Could it be the children's books she'd ordered? She tugged the string and lifted the lid.

And screamed.

Titus tried to listen to Mrs. Holland as she prattled on about the something or other that needed fixing and whether he couldn't stop in and fix it for her. He nodded at all the right spots, guilty for not paying the attention Mrs. Holland deserved.

Of course he could fix whatever had broken. When not working as a deputy, he was the resident handyman around town, always fixing something for somebody, especially for the older ladies or gents who shouldn't be getting up on their roofs or repainting second-floor shutters. And with the snow, he was even more aware of when they needed an extra hand.

Usually, he would pay close attention to a conversation, but he couldn't help casting glances back at Ollie. Had his own foot not slipped on the icy street on his way toward her, he might have been able to cushion her fall. But since he hadn't, she'd landed hard, and he worried she had jarred something. Surely, she could have broken her wrist and ankle, snapped her teeth, or rattled her brain in her head. She had seemed disoriented as she raced away from him.

Had she not been so keen to escape his presence, he would have insisted on taking her to the doc. But as usual, she appeared to want to get away from him as fast as possible. So what was left but to let her go? Not that he'd wanted to. He'd had a schoolboy crush on her since the first moment they were paired in reading during the second grade. He could have listened to her read all afternoon that day. Of course, he'd had to take his turn at reading as the teacher instructed, but reading was not his strong suit. Still wasn't. He could build things—and stories were fun—but reading was boring. Very, very boring.

Maybe that's why Ollie didn't like him. He didn't think her profession was odd, strange, or useless. It was very good for other people to use the library. Maybe he would win her over if he were a library patron.

"You aren't paying attention to a word I said." Fortunately, Mrs. Holland laughed. "Watching the pretty young lady, are you?"

Titus felt embarrassment touch his cheeks. "She took a tumble, and I wanted to ensure she wasn't suffering any ill effects."

"Uh-huh." Mrs. Holland shook her head. He recognized a matchmaking look when he saw one.

"How about I stop by tomorrow morning to fix whatever it is that you need me to fix?" Might as well be honest that he hadn't actually been paying attention.

Mrs. Holland laughed again, then wagged her finger at him. "All right, young man, I will let you get off this once. But this conversation is not over."

Titus bowed. It was most definitely over. People had been trying to set him up with their daughters and their granddaughters and their nieces for years, and he'd parried as much as he could because there was only one girl ... the one who never actually looked at him.

Was he drawn to Ollie because she played hard to get? No, not *played*. Her actions betrayed no game, no attempt at being coy. She was, plain and simple, hard to get because try as he might he couldn't get her to pay attention to him. Was that why he liked her? No. He'd had this ridiculous crush for years. Someday, he would need to grow out of it, especially if she continued to ignore him. He would never force her to pay attention to him if she had no desire to be in his company. That was her prerogative, and he needed to abide by it.

However, it saddened his heart. His shoulders bowed as he turned away from the post office to return across the street. The only reason he had left the jailhouse was to say hi to Ollie, and now he prepared himself for the ribbing that his friend, Casper Yarward, would most certainly give him.

As he stepped into the street, a cry of terror caused him to execute a quick pivot, his hand going to the gun he kept holstered at his waist. It took a blink to register who had screamed and for him to speed down the block that separated them.

Ollie backed away from the library steps, her face white as the snow. He braced his pistol with his left hand as he put himself between her and whatever danger she faced. Heaven help him if it was a rodent or—worse—a child playing a prank on the spinster librarian. He angled the muzzle above the door just in case.

CHAPTER TWO

T he box." Ollie's shaky whisper came from behind his right elbow.

A brown box lay open on the library steps. He cautiously approached it, lowering his pistol but not his guard. A simple peek inside showed him why she'd screamed. His jaw clenched as he holstered his pistol. She needed him calm like a deputy should be, not angry like a man who wished to protect her from something so scarring.

With a long breath to release his tension, he turned, ready to ...

As soon as he saw her broken expression, any thought of what he *should* do left him. She stood trembling in the middle of the road, her arms wrapped around her middle, tears silently falling down her cheeks.

"Oh, Ollie."

He wasn't sure who moved first, but in the next moment, he held her, one hand pressing her head against his chest, the other rubbing small circles along her back. Then her silent tears turned to sobs, and he tightened his hold.

Why would someone mail a dead pheasant to the library? How ... creepy and disgusting and horrid. He grew up on a farm and had helped his father hunt for their family's food, so he understood animal death. But this? This was cruelty of the vilest form. Then, for Ollie to have to see it? He'd never forget walking home with her after school one autumn day, trying to get up the nerve to ask her to the fall dance and instead stumbling upon a fox eating its supper. Ollie had vomited and sobbed and swore she'd never take the forest path again. And he'd made sure she never had to, because that was also the day he lost his heart to her.

Oh sure, he'd been smitten with her since the second grade, but she'd always shied away from him. He'd hoped to change her mind that day. Instead, she'd experienced a trauma, and he'd fallen head over heels. Since he never quite knew whether she was interested in him, and he wasn't willing to risk hurting her, he tried to keep things as platonic as possible. Anytime he tried to cross that line, she ran away.

Why did it have to take a dead pheasant to have the chance to hold her? He rested his chin on her hair. "Ollie, I'll take care of it. You don't have to—"

She jumped away from him, fear in her eyes. "D-did you ... did you s-send it?"

Titus's jaw dropped. "Why would I send you a dead bird? I know how much it hurts you to see an animal suffer. I would never ..." His defensive words trailed off as she buried her face in her hands.

Gently, he urged her toward the security of the library, edged her around the offending delivery, and helped her sit in one of the highback chairs inside. She'd stopped crying as they went, but she wouldn't look at him. Based on the red on her cheeks, her question had embarrassed her.

"Ollie?" He knelt before her. "You had a fright. Of course, you would question the only person within sight. You needed to be reassured." He shouldn't have defended himself. It hadn't been about him, and had he been treating the moment as a civil servant, as a deputy, and not as a man who liked a girl, he wouldn't have embarrassed her.

She nodded. "Why would somebody ... Why would they send it to me?"

"I don't know, Ollie, but I'll try to find out. Please know it wasn't me. I would never, ever do that, especially to you."

She touched his sleeve for a brief moment, her mouth moving without a sound.

"How about I take the box and bury it properly." The ground in the woods should be insulated enough that he could still dig a deep hole this early in the winter. If not, he'd find stones to cover it. For Ollie, he'd do anything.

"I'd like that." Finally. Finally! She raised her gaze to his. "Thank you, Titus."

Then her cheeks flamed scarlet, and she disappeared between the bookshelves without a goodbye.

Titus dropped the offending package on Casper's desk without bothering to remove his winter coat. "Somebody left a dead bird on the library steps."

Casper looked up at him. "And the hero went in to save the day?"

Titus scowled. "This isn't a joke. It scared her to death."

Casper sobered. "All right, all right. Library steps. Are you sure it was for her and not the library?"

"No, I don't know anything at the moment. But we need to investigate it."

"You're right." Casper leaned back in his chair. "Since it happened at the library, and the library is city property and within the jurisdiction of the county ..."

"Oh, stop." Titus dropped into the chair opposite Casper's. "Just tell me you want me to investigate it."

Casper sighed, and Titus massaged his eyes with his thumb and forefinger. His boss had been distracted all morning, and here, Titus was taking his frustration out on him.

He looked at his boss, his friend. "Has Eira Mae had her appointment yet this morning?

Casper shook his head. "I have to head over there in about ten minutes. I mean, she should be okay, right? Having babies ... people have babies all the time, right?

On any other day, Titus would have chuckled at his friend's discomfiture. After the emotion that rocketed through him when Ollie screamed? He couldn't crack a joke. "Do you think there's something wrong?"

"No. Yes." Casper rubbed his face. "Give me a criminal to take down, and—usually—I can do fine. And it's not fatherhood. I'm already a father. Lewis is my child, even if he is not mine by birth. I love being a dad, but I don't like watching Eira Mae go through this. She's so dratted uncomfortable."

Titus smiled. "You would take it from her, wouldn't you?"

Casper raised a brow. "We aren't talking about Eira Mae, are we?"

Heat crept up his neck. "No, I suppose we're not. But Ollie can barely look at me. Man, she ran away from me when I went out to say hello. How am I supposed to call on her, see her, even talk to her if she won't talk to me?"

Casper clasped his hands at his waist, elbows on the arms of his chair. "Perhaps this investigation will give you just the opportunity you need for her to see you as a capable investigator."

"That's just the problem. I think that's all she sees me as. First, I was only a school chum and then only a deputy. I don't think she spoke to me the entire year I was sheriff. Perhaps I intimidated her or something?

"That is a dilemma." A teasing spark brightened his countenance. Then his gaze fell on the box. "Begin by asking questions. See if you can find out why this package was left on her step. See if it's about her or the library, and then we can go from there."

"All right." Titus rose, the plan settling his mind. "Oh, I need to stop by Mrs. Holland's next week. I forgot tomorrow is Sunday, and she's got something she needs me to fix."

"No problem." Casper stood, knocking his knuckles on the top of his desk. "Speaking of that, there was a leak in the cabin roof last time we were up there. If it snows again ... I think I patched it, but if it snows again ..."

Titus swallowed a chuckle. "You want me to look at it?"

Casper kept his attention on his desk. "I can but—"

"You don't want to leave Eira Mae." Titus wouldn't want to leave the woman he loved if there was any risk to her or their unborn child. He could almost feel Ollie in his arms again and pushed the thought away.

"Yeah." Casper shrugged. "I know she'd be fine with my aunt, but ..."

"I get it." He did, even if it made the longing he harbored ache even more. "You don't want to risk getting snowed in while she's down here."

Casper nodded, then squared his shoulders. "I don't want to risk you getting snowed in up there either, but you're right."

"It's the least I can do, Casper." No one would miss him if he got snowed in. He could risk it. And Mr. Osborn, Ollie's grandfather, was the cabin's closest neighbor. He could check on the old hermit while he was up the hill.

"Which brings me to another question." Casper pulled Titus's attention back to him. "How would you feel if we hired another deputy?"

"Probably wise." Titus removed his coat now that he'd warmed enough since coming inside. "I mean, the area is growing. You're going to be a dad of two, and you've already given me more responsibility this past year than before Eira Mae and Lewis became part of your life."

"That's because I know you can handle it." Casper leaned a hip against his desk. "I don't want you to feel that I am replacing you. I'm not. But I took your job, and now I'm hiring somebody else."

That's what this was about. "I don't feel that way. I am not interested in being the sheriff. It was too much, and I didn't enjoy it. I am glad you are the sheriff, Casper. That's the honest truth. I am glad to be your right hand. Leave me with that position, and I am perfectly content in my career."

"Are you sure?"

Titus rolled his eyes and snatched the box from the desk. "How many times do I have to tell you there are no hard feelings? In fact, I am so glad you're back that had I known Eira Mae could convince you to return, I would have somehow found a way to bring her to the cabin much sooner and without so much trouble."

"All right, all right." Casper chuckled. "I believe you."

"Good." Titus huffed. He hated how many people assumed he'd be angry or at least disgruntled that Casper had reclaimed the sheriff's position. They had even wanted him to run against Casper in the election this past November, but he refused. He preferred being a deputy, and he liked working for Casper.

"Keep an eye on her." Casper pointed his chin at the box as he shrugged into his coat. "My gut says that package was meant for Ollie. We need to find out why."

Titus agreed.

"Maybe she'll finally talk to you." Casper grinned, then winked. "Being loved by a good woman makes life worth living."

"Yeah, yeah. Tell Eira Mae hello for me." Titus shook his head as his boss left. He was happy for his friend. Honestly, he was. But Casper's tease hit too close to home. Titus wanted a girl like Casper had found in Eira Mae, and only one had ever fit the picture in his mind.

Titus scrounged up a stack of old newspaper and carefully lifted the bird from the package to prepare it for its ceremony. He hoped this would allow Ollie to lay the trauma to rest just as much as the bird. She had such a quiet, gentle, sensitive soul.

As he settled the bird on the newsprint, a piece of paper fluttered to the ground beside his boot. He lifted it by the corner so as not to smudge the writing, and any question that the package had anything to do with the library vanished.

To my true love: please accept this gift of provision.

Titus turned cold. Ollie had a secret admirer.

CHAPTER THREE

Sunday, December 14
11 days until Christmas

The following morning, Ollie woke to a world blanketed in white. While the sun remained hidden behind gray clouds, the fresh coating covered the dirt, mud, and memories of the day before—not all the memories, just the bad ones. She could still feel the comfort she'd received as Titus tended to her.

Of course, she had to ruin it by accusing him of leaving the package. Fear had run away with her tongue.

Nevertheless, she hadn't doubted his reason for postponing the bird burial last afternoon—a broken fence had allowed a herd of cows to block a road—but a part of her wondered whether she'd effectively pushed him away forever. However, the delay caused her to realize it would be better to offer the pheasant as a gift to a family needing supper than to bury it simply out of her sensitivities. It was better to multiply gifts rather than bury them in the ground. So she sent a note around to Titus to deliver it to whom he thought best.

The cold air hurried along her preparations she readied for Sunday Church. She heard her landlady, Mrs. Clark, moving around downstairs as well as the other woman who rented a room across the hall. Since Ollie was among the few residents left—Eira Mae had been a resident before she married Casper at the beginning of the year—Mrs. Clark often talked about whether to allow married couples or families to live there because she had to earn a living, too. It was the reason she'd opened the boardinghouse in the first place. She wanted to help women who had no choice but to work for their food.

Ollie slipped into her Mary Janes and hurried down the stairs. The savory scent of whatever Mrs. Clark planned for Sunday Dinner wafted from the kitchen. Mrs. Clark's late husband was a state gamekeeper for Wisconsin's wildlife conservation and management, so his widow was well-versed in cooking game meat and what animals had to be protected. Ollie usually appreciated Mrs. Clark's protective streak, but today, the cooking smells reminded her too much of the package left on the library steps last night.

So, instead of greeting her landlady as she usually did, or staying for breakfast, Ollie donned her coat and silently slipped out the front door. She turned to descend the porch steps and tripped over a small white box.

Her heart hammered as she picked it up. Bound with twine, it fit in the palm of her hand. With trembling fingers, she turned over the brown tag.

To: Olivia

From: Your True Love

Nausea made her grateful she'd foregone breakfast. She could not reenter the house and hold down the contents of her stomach.

Casper and Eira Mae had a house on the outskirts of town that once belonged to baby Lewis's late parents. Too far to walk with how her legs shook.

Could she take this to Titus? He lived above the jailhouse. Alone. No. That was highly improper. She'd have to wait to see him at church. Not that she could work up the courage to say hi—she never did.

Mrs. Clark would help her if she could just go back inside. The very thought made her gag. What about Mrs. Holland? She and Mrs. Clark were friends, and Mrs. Holland had been speaking to Titus yesterday. Surely, she could help Ollie or telephone someone who could. Like Titus.

Relief strengthened her wobbly legs. She tugged the offending package into her pocket and forced herself not to run to Manitowish Waters Inn.

With his head wedged behind the wood stove, Titus could barely hear Mrs. Holland's continual apologies.

He'd been mostly dressed for church when the older woman had telephoned in a panic. Instead of changing, he grabbed work clothes and hustled to the Inn. Fortunately, the problem wasn't an emergency, allowing him to change before getting covered in ashes.

He brushed his blackened hands on his trousers and crawled out from behind the stove. "Everything looks okay."

"But you saw the smoke." Mrs. Holland waved her hands in the air before returning to wringing them. "I knew the stove wasn't working properly. That's what I mentioned to you yesterday."

When he hadn't listened well. His neck heated.

"But baking biscuits this morning, the stove pillowed black smoke." Mrs. Holland's voice quivered. "I always offer a complimentary breakfast to my guests. What will I do without a stove? I cannot afford to fix it, much less replace it."

"Mrs. Holland." He tugged her fingers free of the tangle she'd gotten them in, and despite their filthiness, she didn't pull away. "That's why you telephoned."

She turned glassy eyes up at him. "But you said everything was okay."

Titus smiled, tenderness welling for this widow under his care. "And you didn't let me finish."

She huffed, then grinned. "I suppose we're even then, deputy."

Titus laughed. "I suppose we are. And I am happy to help. I'm sure your guests won't mind having a cold breakfast if they can't wait."

"You think you can fix it?" The *that soon* was left unsaid, but Titus heard it nonetheless.

He shrugged on his coat. "Something is causing the smoke, but I'm not seeing it from down here. I'll climb up on the roof to see if there's something wrong with the flue, like a bird's nest or other debris."

She sucked in a breath. "I can't let you get on the roof with the snow falling like this."

Titus slapped on his newsboy cap. "Better today than tomorrow when there will be much more of it."

Fortunately, Mrs. Holland let him leave the kitchen without further protest. He found the ladder she kept in her gardener's shack out back and carefully climbed to the roof. The snow made things slippery, but it took only a few minutes to determine he was correct: a bird had built a nest in the chimney pipe.

He cleared the branches, then scrubbed the ash and soot from his hands in the icy water from the pump. If he quickly changed into his Sunday clothes here—or forewent changing altogether—he could still make the start of Sunday services.

However, when he reentered the kitchen, he discovered Ollie sitting at the kitchen table, her face as white as the small box in front of her. Dressed in her Sunday best, she looked pretty as a picture ... until she glanced his way with eyes filled with distress.

"See, Titus is here." Mrs. Holland motioned him to sit beside Ollie at her kitchen table. Remnants of the burnt biscuits were gone, the smoky smell replaced by the scent of pine from the bough that hadn't been on the table when he'd left. Mrs. Holland rubbed Ollie's upper arms. "It will all be okay now, sweetling. I need to help a guest. Titus will take care of you."

Ollie nodded as she whispered her thanks.

Mrs. Holland patted Titus's shoulder, then leaned close to his ear. "I told you we'd revisit a certain conversation. Consider it revisited."

Titus barely—barely!—refrained from rolling his eyes at the older woman. However, as soon as the kitchen door closed behind her, he focused all his attention on Ollie. He hadn't a clue how to help her, though. What type of admirer kept his identity a secret while leaving dead birds for the object of his affection to find?

"Mrs. Holland said you were fixing her oven?" Ollie cast him a furtive glance, the gesture and quiver in her voice reminiscent of how she'd run away from him yesterday. It pierced that he could be worsening her anxiety. Could that be why this other would-be beau resorted to secret gifts? His gut twisted. No wonder she worried that he had sent the pheasant yesterday!

He refused to be anything like this other man. If protecting her peace of mind meant handing over the investigation, he would do so. He steeled his heart against the blow she could wield. "Ollie, do I make you nervous?"

She ducked her chin and nodded.

He forced his shoulder not to sink and willed his fortifications not to crack. "Would you prefer Mrs. Holland stayed while we talk?"

Slowly but clearly, she shook her head.

Okay, good. Titus relaxed a smidgen. Her discomfort didn't have to do with being alone with him. Another thought struck. Did she doubt his investigative skills? He'd heard the rumors since Casper retook the sheriff's position that Titus had failed as sheriff, forcing Casper to return. It's why Casper kept asking whether he was satisfied as a deputy. Could Ollie feel the same?

He swallowed, then forced himself to ask, "Do you want me to call Cas—er, Sheriff Yarwood to take over the investigation?"

Her head shot up. "No!" Then she gasped and clapped both hands over her mouth. Her cheeks turned cherry red. And her eyes widened as she continued to stare at him.

Titus pinned his lips together to contain a smile, his heart tearing down the protections from inside. Ollie Larson didn't mind being alone with him and didn't want anyone else investigating her dilemma. Then maybe, just maybe, she was nervous because she *liked* him. Hope sprung. Perhaps he'd read her signals wrong all these years.

Ollie slowly lowered her hands to the table, where she clasped them tightly together. "I-I didn't mean that the sheriff couldn't investigate. And if y-you want Mrs. Holland here, th-that is fine. I—"

"Ollie." Titus stopped her stammering, which he now saw in a new light. He covered her hands with his. "I'm glad I'm here for you."

Her mouth rounded into an adorable *O*, and he forced himself not to stare. "Tell me about the box?"

She blanched, and he jerked his hand from hers. How brutish could he be?

"I'm sorry, that was abrupt." He bit off the rest of his explanation, realizing he was about to ramble just like Ollie had done.

"It's why I'm here." She used the tip of her finger to slide it toward him. "Open it?"

The trust in her tone comforted him even as the words on the tag chilled him. "Any ideas who left this?"

She shook her head.

"No beau?" He hadn't heard of any callers, not that he'd been paying *that* close attention. But theirs was a small town.

Again, she shook her head.

Good news for his chances with her, bad news for finding the person leaving these packages. He'd heard of the term *erotomania*, a case of someone's deluded belief that the object of their obsession loved them in return.

Often, the erotomaniac—usually a woman—would follow the object of her obsession, even resorting to violence when her love was not returned. Could Ollie have such a person devoted to her?

"Ollie, have you noticed a gentleman who visits the library frequently? Someone who stops to talk with you. Perhaps he's paid a particular kindness?"

Her nose scrunched in concentration. "Many men are patrons of the library. Mr. Klein gives me the day-old papers so patrons who don't visit his barber shop can still read the news. They are all kind to me and talk to me. You think the person leaving these ... gifts is one of them?"

Titus stifled another smile despite the worry in her voice. That was more words than he usually got from her. He forced himself to sober. "I'm glad they are all kind, Ollie. But I need to know if someone is paying you more attention than makes you comfortable."

Her shoulders slumped. "All attention makes me uncomfortable."

It shouldn't make him happy, that information. But it did. It gave him a clue about how to win her over. Of course, the timing couldn't be worse. He shouldn't consider calling on Ollie while discussing an obsessive man who called himself her true love. He'd refrained all these years because she seemed so uneasy around him.

"That was a long sigh. I'm sorry I can't help more."

He deserved a head slap for thinking of himself at such a time. "You're being a perfect help, Ollie."

"Then ..."

He would not answer that. He tapped the tag. "I found a similar note in the box yesterday. This person called himself your true love and sent the bird to provide your dinner."

Her eyebrows pushed together. "That was oddly thoughtful. If misguided." And that was why Titus has always liked Ollie. Hearing her compassion for a man who had terrified her made him admire her all the more.

"Are you ready to see what's inside?" They had to get this over with.

"Will you open it?"

The trust she had in him made him sit up taller. "Ready?"

She shrugged, then brushed imaginary crumbs from the table as he used his pocket knife to cut the twine.

"Huh." Titus stared at the two glass birds nestled in a bed of sticks and straw. "You can look."

"Figurines?" Ollie peered into the box, her soft lavender scent mingling with the pine's strong smell. "I don't understand."

"There's writing on this little stick." Titus tilted the box to see it better and grimaced. *Our home.*

He had no doubt Ollie had caught the eye of an erotomaniac, which meant Titus had to find him before he scarred Ollie's sweet soul or escalated to violence.

Chapter 4
Chapter Four

Monday, December 15
10 days until Christmas

Ollie tugged on her woolen stockings, determined to open the library as usual today. Titus and Casper had both advised against it yesterday, explaining how they thought she might have someone trying to win her affection. How could a gentleman do so if she didn't know who he was?

Anyway, if she wanted the attention of someone, she knew who she'd pick. If only she would stop freezing up or babbling incoherently. At least she'd managed to keep Titus from running yesterday. When Mrs. Holland had told her Titus was fixing her oven, Ollie knew she'd made the right decision to seek help at the Inn.

And Titus wanted to help her.

Ollie bit her lip as she slipped on her Mary Janes. Could he think of her as more than an old schoolmate? Or was she seeing a Prince Charming where she should see a detective hero?

Mrs. Clark called from downstairs, and the censure in her voice warned it had something to do with a boy. Ollie sighed, pushing down whimsical thoughts of gallant detectives saving a damsel in distress, and gathered her coat and purse. Mrs. Clark ran a strict female board-inghouse. No male guests unless properly chaperoned in the parlor.

Yesterday, Titus had offered to escort her to the library. She hated to be a bother, so she'd declined, but what if he'd come by anyway?

She hurried down the steps, only to freeze midway—and nearly lose her footing—when she noted the brown box in Mrs. Clark's hands. Not Titus. Not Titus at all.

"This was left on the porch." Mrs. Clark scowled, shaking the box. "I do not approve of receiving gifts from an unknown gentleman."

Ollie couldn't move, couldn't breathe. "D-do y-you know who d-dropped it off?"

Mrs. Clark narrowed her eyes, her frown evening into a thin line. "This wasn't the reaction I expected. Come down here, child."

Ollie's knees began to tremble, her hands, too. She didn't dare let go of the railing, or she would land in a heap at the bottom of the steps.

Mrs. Clark set the package on the entry table and met Ollie on the stairs. "Come sit in the parlor before you tumble down the stairs in a faint. I'll telephone the sheriff."

Would Casper tell Titus? Nothing against Eira Mae's husband, but Titus was her friend. He made her feel nervous, yes, but also so very safe.

Mrs. Clark settled Ollie in the parlor and closed the doors. At first, Ollie wanted to reopen them, needing to know she wasn't alone. However, upon hearing the other boarder descend the steps, likely headed to her teller position at the bank, she was glad Mrs. Clark had provided the privacy. Ollie struggled to keep from breathing too hard and fast, let alone find enough air to explain anything.

Not a quarter of an hour later, Titus burst into the parlor with Casper on his heels, both with their sheriff stars displayed on the lapels of their uniform suits. They wore matching grim expressions, though Titus offered her a tight smile.

Mrs. Clark brought the box and unceremoniously set it in Casper's hands. "Must you open that in front of her?"

Casper cast Ollie a sympathetic smile. "Unfortunately, yes. We need her permission to open it. However, Ollie, I would advise you to allow us to look inside first."

"Please." Ollie blinked away her tears.

Mrs. Clark wrapped a motherly arm around Ollie while they watched the men. Titus shifted, blocking her view of the box Casper held in his palms, and lifted the lid. Simultaneous sighs followed the lowering of their shoulders.

"It's not an animal exactly." Titus turned to them. "But it's not anything hard to see."

"You think it's from this same person? The one you said left her these other packages?" Mrs. Clark demanded, tugging Ollie closer. "Who would leave gifts of this sort on a young woman's doorstep without proper introduction?"

"We aim to find out, Mrs. Clark." Casper brought the box to them, kneeling so that Ollie and Mrs. Clark could see inside.

"Eggs?" Ollie's voice squeaked.

"And why three of them?" Mrs. Clark muttered. She rubbed Ollie's arm. "Tell me again what he left her the past two days?"

"A pheasant." Casper, thankfully, left off the *dead* part.

"And glass doves," Titus added.

"Pheasant, doves, and these eggs look like they come from a common Leghorn layer." Mrs. Clark tapped her chin.

Ollie rubbed her temples. "I'm sorry I'm no help. It's as if someone has washed the pages of my mind, and the ink has run into one big smear."

"Brilliant." Titus snapped his fingers as he dropped to his knees beside the sheriff. "We need to look for a note."

"Pheasant, dove, eggs," Mrs. Clark muttered as the men carefully set the eggs on the floor to dig through what appeared to be a nest.

"See, Ollie?" Titus winked at her, and she covered her warm cheeks with her hands. "You did help."

"Pheasant, doves, eggs ... " Mrs. Clark continued to mutter. "Pheasant, doves, laying eggs."

"There is a note." Casper lifted the white paper. "*Laying hens for our new home, amour.*"

"*Amour*?" Ollie croaked. Was this person going to ruin the language of romance for her? *Les Misérables, The Count of Monte Cristo, Beauty and the Beast ...*

"What does *amour* mean?" Titus halted her spiraling thoughts

"French for *love*." Mrs. Clark waved her hand as if that was entirely beside the point. "French and eggs. Two doves. And a par—ohh ... I have a bad feeling, gentlemen."

"What?" Casper set the note and box aside.

"You know my late husband worked for the Wisconsin State Conservation Commission?"

"Yes, ma'am." Casper nodded. "Gamekeeper, basically."

"Well, he taught me a lot about the animals who live in our lovely state, and the partridge is not native to Wisconsin. Pheasant is."

"What does a partridge ..." Titus's question trailed off, and his face paled.

"The song?" Ollie was grateful she had yet to have breakfast, or she might cast it up.

"One pheasant. Two doves." Casper pointed to the eggs. "Three ... hens?"

"French hens." Titus dragged a hand over his face. "My fear from yesterday isn't as outlandish as it seemed. Whoever sent you these gifts is calling himself your true love. He means to make you his wife."

"My true ... His ..." Ollie's stomach heaved.

"Gentlemen, perhaps we can continue this later," Mrs. Clark fussed, drawing a blanket over Ollie's trembling shoulders. "I know you need more information to catch this reprobate, but not at Ollie's expense. I must insist you give her a moment to recover. This is too much for her."

Ollie wanted to protest, but she wanted to curl up in a ball more.

"With all due respect, ma'am." Casper stood. "We can't find this person unless we know who has been paying Ollie undue attention."

"But we don't have to ask that now, do we?" Titus rose so that he blocked her view of Casper. "Your wife has another appointment this morning. Go home. With Mrs. Clark's permission, I'll stay and keep watch. We'll reconvene after the lunch hour."

Ollie's head sank onto the arm of the sofa as Titus's defense wrapped her in a cocoon of safety. His strong voice as he stood up to his boss—for her—was what heroes were made of. This package-leaving person didn't understand the word.

"Alright." Casper sighed. "I'll take the eggs and note back to the office."

"And I'll get Titus a cup of coffee." Mrs. Clark lifted Ollie's feet onto the sofa and tucked the blanket around her. "Some cocoa for you, too, child. It always helps with a fright."

Tears burned Ollie's eyes at the kindness of her landlady. "Thank you, Mrs. Clark."

"One more thing." Mrs. Clark halted Casper's exit with the box. "Ollie planned to visit her grandfather for Christmas. I think she should leave today."

Ollie wanted to disagree, to insist she had to keep the library open, but hiding away at her grandfather's isolated cabin sounded like the perfect remedy.

"Wise," Casper said. "Titus, can you escort her?"

"Absolutely." Not a hint of hesitation. "While I'm there, I'll check on your cabin roof since it snowed."

"Then it's settled." Mrs. Clark's heels clicked from the room, followed by a heavier tread. Ollie's eyes drifted closed.

"Ollie?" Titus knelt beside her, hand on her shoulder. "Is that plan alright with you?"

Her eyelids fluttered open to find his blue ones startlingly close. Words dried on her tongue, but she nodded. There was no other person she trusted more to see her safely to her grandfather's cabin.

Dare she wish for a snowstorm to keep Titus close by, like what happened to Eira Mae?

CHAPTER FIVE

Tuesday, December 16
9 days until Christmas

Titus woke to a dripping sound in Casper's cabin. The air had a distinct chill that made his nose cold, and he wished he could stay under the warm quilt. However, the *plunk* of water meant the morning was warm enough to melt snow from the roof. If Titus acted quickly, perhaps he could find the leak that much faster.

Taking a moment to shove his legs into his trousers and don a flannel shirt over his long johns, he strained his ears for the location of the dripping. The sound seemed to bounce around the room—or did it originate from the main room? He'd left the bedroom door open to allow heat from the wood stove to keep him warm overnight.

He paused his search to kneel before the stove. He stoked the coals, then added wood. *Plunk.* The sound was louder here than in the bedroom. He filled the kettle with water from the bucket beside the stove. The lack of ice covering the water's surface confirmed the warmer temperature.

While the fire heated both the kettle and the room, Titus continued roving about. He remained in his socks, hoping his feet might hit a wet spot on the plank floor while he craned his neck to search the ceiling. The single room contained a stove, a table with chairs, a couple of rockers, a bookcase, and a fireplace. The roof had a low peak down the center of the room, with rafters supporting it. There was not enough room for a second story.

Two years ago, a failed arrest had led Titus to kill a man in self-defense. Casper thought it his fault and had moved to the cabin as penance, leaving Titus serving as sheriff and wishing Casper would return. However, in the year Casper had lived out here like a hermit, he'd made the place habitable. Titus recognized the improvements, including the ones his boss had made over the summer months when he and Eira Mae escaped town as a family. With their adopted son, Lewis, toddling around, Casper had added fencing with narrow spacing between posts and rails. The stone path to the outdoor privy was also new. All-in-all, it held a homey quality Titus hadn't noted before.

Except Casper and his family lived in town and only visited the cabin occasionally, which would explain the roof leak. No one had been here to catch the damage before it worsened. Titus would have to check the floor where the water landed to be sure no boards had rotted. It wouldn't do to have Lewis or Eira Mae get hurt because he hadn't done the job properly.

He noticed no dripping in the middle of the room, so he moved to the edges. He first checked the south and west sides since the added-on bedroom was attached there. The seams had held, and the bedroom was dry. The water in the kettle warned it would boil soon, so Titus quickly searched the east wall, guessing he'd find the leak along the north side of the house. He let the kettle whistle as he neared the northeast corner. Nothing yet ... *Plunk*. A drop of icy water splashed his nose.

"Found it," Titus said aloud, though he was alone. He couldn't see the damage without a ladder, so he dug up a pot to catch the water. After he had his coffee, fed his horse, and checked on Ollie and her grandfather, he'd climb up to see what had caused the problem. Hopefully, it was fixable without walking on the snow-covered roof, but he didn't hold out much hope of avoiding that.

Titus had also volunteered to fix the roof simply so Casper wouldn't need to. Eira Mae needed Casper with all working limbs. No one needed ... the thought faded from Titus's mind as he sipped his coffee. Ollie needed him to stay in one piece so he could protect her. He couldn't do that laid up with a broken leg or a smashed-in skull.

He tapped his finger against the side of his mug. If he couldn't repair the roof without stepping foot on it, he'd cajole Osborn into being his spotter. At least if he fell, then he wouldn't freeze to death in the snow. Just the thought urged him outside to finish his chores so he could see Ollie all the sooner. And in no time, he pushed thoughts of the roof repair out of his mind and headed for Osborn's place.

Osborn's cabin was only accessible by foot or horse; even a wagon would have trouble through the trees. Casper's cabin, too, but less so. He and Titus had plans for next summer to carve a path that would make the Yarwood cabin more accessible, so Casper could take his family up to the cabin more comfortably. And as Casper's uncle, the judge, and his wife aged, a wagon or even one of those newfangled automobiles would make much more sense for them.

But Osborn's cabin?

Titus finished his coffee, then shrugged on his coat. The path between Casper's cabin and Osborn's was nothing more than a deer path. With the snow—he snagged the pair of snowshoes Casper kept beside the front door—he'd had to take the path down and around the hill last night. Today, he'd be prepared.

He shoved the ends of the snowshoes in the snow outside the barn door, then greeted his horse. From what Titus heard, Casper had gotten along famously with Osborn because they left each other alone. Of course, they were neighborly if they needed each other, even friendly if they needed one to look after the other's property. Not that Osborn ever left his place.

In no time, Titus finished caring for his horse, strapped on the snowshoes, and made his way up the hill. Going around would be easier, barely, but this way would be less visible and more direct. A horse could traverse it in the summer. However, in the winter, snowshoes barely made it passable.

Like the way to Casper's cabin, the path from the main road to Osborn's place wasn't wide enough for a wagon. However, since Osborn rarely left his secluded place, even Titus's horse had struggled with it last night. Ollie had tried to insist on letting her traverse it alone, to spare the horse, bless her sweet soul. But Titus wouldn't hear of it.

The thought of seeing her, assuring himself of her safety, had him increasing his pace. Soon, sweat trickled down his back beneath his heavy coat. It was a recipe for illness, but the strenuous path left too much time for his mind to run wild.

Osborn's cabin was the perfect place for Ollie to hide out. It was hard to find and access, and he doubted most knew the connection between her and her grandfather. Even if they shared the same surname, Osborn's reclusive nature kept him out of sight and out of mind.

However, the isolated nature of the two cabins—Casper's and Osborn's—caused Titus to wonder if this was indeed the smartest move. Second-guessing the decision had kept him up half the night. Last year, he and Judge Cavenaugh sent Eira Mae here to hide out, but they'd sent her to Casper. Osborn was handy with a shotgun, but Titus wasn't there to protect her.

Progressive times allowed a man and a woman to be alone in a room or a vehicle together. However, even with Osborn as a chaperone, Titus couldn't invite himself to stay overnight, especially without a credible physical threat.

Osborn's chimney came into view, the smoke rising above the trees shielding the house. Secluded, but not defendable. Was Ollie in physical danger from this man who thought her his true love? Was he a true erotomaniac who would resort to violence if he didn't get Ollie, or would he move on when he realized Ollie wasn't interested?

Titus worked to slow his heart and breathing after the exerting walk, but his angst only rose. He knew he felt possessively protective because he cared about Ollie. Did he see shadows where there were none because of it? See a deranged individual instead of a common rival?

Staying at Casper's was far enough away, but as soon as Titus fixed the roof, he would need to return to town. Casper had an interview today with a potential deputy, and he wanted Titus to meet him. Titus wanted to stall, but he had no excuse. His job of escorting Ollie safely to her grandfather's had been completed.

Ollie sat at her grandfather's kitchen table, feet tucked under her, gaze pinned to the front door as she sipped her morning coffee. Grandfather had urged her to join him outside for chores, but Ollie declined. She never missed a moment in Grandfather's company, and her decision ate at her. But what if her unwelcome gift-giver had left another package on the doorstep?

It was irrational, she knew. The person didn't know where to find her, nor was her life in danger. Yet even spending an hour in Grandfather's company couldn't calm the fear that this person would follow her here. Perhaps even with a gift more horrible than the first. She shivered. Why had God given her such an imagination? It served her well as a librarian, but not ... today.

The front door opened, sending a blast of cold snow into the warm kitchen. Ollie jerked, her coffee splashing onto the table.

"Grandfather!" Ollie pressed her hand to her pounding heart.

"You're awful jumpy." Grandfather shut the door as he stomped snow from his boots.

Ollie set her cup on the worn table with a huff. "I shouldn't be." Perhaps the only way not to be was to find out who left those ... packages.

To call them gifts chilled her even more than the cold outside. She fished the dishrag from the tepid dishwater and wiped the spill off the table. Fortunately, the coffee had missed her dress. It was her warmest, but that wasn't why she chose to wear it today. The rose-patterned cotton was serviceable and comfortable, yes, but it also made her feel pretty. And she needed to feel good about herself. The person who gave her those ... things ... left her feeling ... discomfited.

"Hmmm." The rusty vibration in Grandfather's voice showed how little he used it. "Yer not one to overreact. This gent did a number on ya."

Ollie dropped the dishrag into the wash water. "You don't think he'll find me here, do you?" *Please say no.* Neither Casper nor Titus had offered such solace. Perhaps Grandfather would. Not that she'd believe him.

Grandfather hung his coat, then approached her slowly, gently, as he would an injured sparrow. "I say we get through Christmas Day, then his game will be done."

Ollie nodded, but her Grandfather's calm tone didn't comfort her as it usually did.

Grandfather turned her away from the washbasin, his gnarled hands on her shoulders. He smelled of his particular brand of pipe tobacco mixed with the pine that isolated his property. Her short stature meant his long gray beard tickled her nose.

She wrapped her arms around his thin waist. "I'm scared."

Sound rumbled in his chest. "I suppose, if this gent were to find you here, we'd scare him off with my shotgun."

Ollie gave a watery chuckle. Grandfather tended to shoot the thing before asking questions. Yet could bring an injured animal back from the brink of death.

He rubbed her back. "At any sign of mischief, you could always stay at Casper's cabin with that lawman of his."

"Grandfather!" Ollie leapt from Grandfather's embrace and slapped her hands to her cheeks as her body heated to what had to be an unsafe level. "That would be highly inappropriate!"

Grandfather shrugged, then tugged off his knit cap, and his wild gray mane underscored his reclusive tendencies. Did he not remember any civilities or social rules that could ruin a girl's life? Apparently not. He offered no apology for such an outlandish idea.

"You need a haircut." Ollie made a mental note to give him one before she returned to town, whenever that would be. "Anyway, Titus is not planning to stay at Casper's cabin for long. I heard he's returning to town as soon as he repairs the roof. So you see, that is not an option."

So much for changing the subject.

"He told you that, did he?" Grandfather tracked her return to the table for her coffee with hawkish eyes. "Hmm. Yes, I believe I see quite well. And I disagree. He sounded awfully worried last night."

Ollie picked up her cup, careful not to spill it again. "Of course, he's worried about me. He's a deputy. He worries about everyone." Though her heart gave an extra beat in the hope that Grandfather might be right.

"I wouldn't be so sure about that." Grandfather cocked his head.

Ollie opened her mouth to protest when someone pounded on the front door. A scream jumped up her throat before she could clamp her lips shut, and her cup flew from her hands. The next moment, Titus stood in the doorway, pistol raised, gaze searching the cabin until they landed on her.

Grandfather laughed.

"Are you all right?" Titus kicked the door shut with his heel and holstered his weapon before slowly approaching her. He glanced at Grandfather—who was still chuckling—but kept his fiery concentration primarily on her.

The intensity of it mixed with her relief, so that she began to tremble. First her hands, then her arms. Down to her knees, then up her back. She covered her face, embarrassed but unable to stop shaking, nor the tears that dripped down her cheeks, not even the giggle. Was she going mad?

"Ollie, sweetie, sit, please. You're worrying me." Titus's voice was low in her ear as he guided her to a chair, his words just for her. Then louder, he said. "Did I miss something? Is something wrong?"

Grandfather's woodsy scent wrapped around her from behind. Titus had a timbery smell, too. But not wild like Grandfather. More ... civilized. She snorted. Oh, what was she thinking? The ridiculousness of her thoughts caused more laughter to bubble up.

"Osborn?" The concern in Titus's voice cut through her hysteria.

"I'm fine." Ollie groaned. "I think I am. But maybe not. I'm just glad that you're here. I mean, that it was you. And not the other person. Oh, please help me stop talking."

Titus knelt beside her, taking her hands in his. Both sets were cold, yet warmth spread to her heart. "It's going to be alright, Ollie. You don't have to be afraid."

"Mmhmm," Grandfather mumbled from behind. "I see right fine."

CHAPTER SIX

Titus breathed easier now that he was sure there was no danger in Osborn's house. Color had returned to Ollie's cheeks, though that might be because of her grandfather. Titus had seen enough match-making relatives to recognize the look in Osborn's eye. Not that he minded in this particular case.

"Do you have any news for us?" Osborn seated himself across the table.

Titus stood from where he'd been kneeling in front of Ollie. "No, I'm sorry, I don't. Once I fix Casper's roof I will head into town again to continue the investigation. I aim to return by the end of the day."

"Then why are you here?" Osborn stared at him.

"Grandfather!" Ollie jumped to her feet, nearly knocking Titus off balance as she brushed by him. "It's okay for a neighbor to visit once in a while. You don't need to run everybody off."

Osborn raised his chin. "I like my solitude."

Titus shuffled to his feet. He didn't want to leave Ollie, but even more so after witnessing her fright. In fact, just the thought of going back to Casper's cabin set a stone in his gut. Obviously, she was on edge and he wanted to be here for her.

However, he wouldn't get in between Ollie and her grandfather. He cleared his throat. "If it's an inconvenience for me to be here ..."

"It is not an inconvenience," Ollie snapped, then spun toward the stove. "I'll get you a cup of coffee and then you have every reason to sit down at the table. Grandfather, you can make him feel welcome."

Osborn turned his chin away from his granddaughter and gave Titus a wink.

Titus rolled his eyes as he took an empty chair. Despite his lack of hospitality, Osborn had four of them, though there was no other seating in the small cabin. "I would be happy to stay for coffee, Ollie."

An awkward silence descended on the cabin as Ollie returned to her chair. Titus wasn't sure how to change that. His words dried up as the adrenaline left his body. Osborn sure didn't help. He contentedly drank his coffee, alternately watching Titus and Ollie. Ollie kept her gaze strictly on her coffee. Titus stifled a sigh. He would need to figure out what to say, but the only thing he could think to discuss was the dratted boxes. It was all he and Ollie had in common.

He sipped his coffee. If the case was all they had to say to each other, then what hope of a future could he have? They needed more than a stranger leaving her gifts. There had to be something else. He could ask her questions, perhaps talk about the library, but what did he know? He couldn't remember the last time he had stepped inside. Perhaps that was his mistake. Could he have won her over so much sooner as a patron?

Then again, why would he go into the library? He didn't read because books were boring. He didn't need a newspaper because he and Casper got all the news he could handle. Titus did not need to know what other crimes were happening in the country when he had enough of it in their own county. Nor did he need to know which society lady was visiting some town or another. If he wanted such gossip, he could stop Mrs. Clark or Mrs. Holland on the sidewalk and ask.

So where did that leave him in coming up with something to talk about? Was he nervous because Osborn was eyeing him, daring him to open his mouth? And what did it say for Titus's courage if he couldn't muster it to actually *say something* to the girl he admired?

Titus cleared his throat. "Did you bring a book with you?" It seemed a ridiculous question now that he spoke it aloud.

However, it must have been the right one because Ollie looked up with a smile of joy brightening her face. "I did! When we stopped by the library to lock up before we left last afternoon, and you opened that package for me? I brought those books with me."

"They were children's books, right? They looked illustrated." Titus had felt very protective when she'd handed him the box to open and very relieved to find the book she'd ordered inside with no evidence of a note from the man who thought he was her true love.

Ollie was nodding. "I purchased *Benjamin Bunny* for a couple of the schoolboys who visit the library. They're the most adorable stories about these mischievous bunnies who get into all sorts of mischief. Have you read any of Miss Potter's books?"

"No, but I wish I—" He stopped. Did he wish he had, or was he saying that because he wanted to keep a smile on Ollie's lips? The check had him realizing that he truly wished he'd read them because, if he had, he would be able to talk to Ollie about them. Titus turned his coffee cup, feeling his cheeks heat. "I don't really read, but hearing you talk about those books ... they sound interesting."

"I brought *A Tale of Peter Rabbit* with me, too. It's the first book. Would you like to borrow it?"

"Oh, I couldn't take one of your books." Titus felt the heat spreading from his cheeks to the rest of him. "I mean, I have to return to town tonight after I fix the roof. Speaking of which ... Osborn, can you be my spotter? I have to fix the leak in Casper's cabin and I need to get up on the roof, and I ... sorry, let me try that again."

Osborn laughed, and Titus wished to crawl under the table. But Ollie grinned.

"I would be happy to send the book with you." Then her smile faded. "What's this about getting on a roof? Mrs. Clark was very worried when you got up on the roof the other day. There's much more snow now, especially here in the forest. Can't it wait?"

Osborn straightened in his chair. "She's right. You shouldn't be up on a roof in this weather."

"I agree." Titus willed his embarrassment back under control. "However, if I let the leak go unfixed while nobody stays at the cabin, it will only worsen and potentially cause permanent damage. I need to patch it to at least get us through until the snow thaws, and I can't do that from inside. Osborn, if you could hold the ladder for me, that would be an extra level of safety."

"No." Ollie stood. "If you get on the roof, even with someone there, and you fall, you could be seriously injured. We are so far from a doctor, from help. You can't get on the roof, Titus. You can't."

Titus reveled in her obvious concern for him. "I promise I plan to be careful, Ollie. I won't actually step on the roof if I can help it. I believe the leak is closer to the corner. That means I should be able to keep my feet on the ladder. And with your grandfather holding it steady, I should be just fine."

Ollie huffed. "Take your life in your hands, then. I don't want to be there to watch you break your neck." She ran for her coat and disappeared outside before she had even put it on.

Titus rose to go after her, but Osborn stopped him. "You know why she is overreacting, right?"

"Of course. She's been through a lot these last few days. Her nerves are overextended. Why shouldn't she react?"

Osborn grunted. "You aren't half as smart as I thought you were. The woman cares about you, Wilburn. If you get hurt, it would devastate her. Now, what do you plan to do about it?"

"I can't do anything until—"

"You mean you won't do anything. What does your job description say about *can't*?"

Titus paused. Would it be okay to mix his job of protecting Ollie with the possibility of seeing where a relationship could go? "She has this other person who wants her attention. I won't be compared to him. I won't push her."

"Which is the point." Osborn glared at him. "She needs someone to show her what True Love really is. And the way you stormed into this cabin when you thought she could be in trouble? Well, there was nothing at all about your entrance that had anything to do with your job."

Titus swallowed. He hated to admit that the old man was right.

"Now get. Talk to her, then we'll both help you fix that roof."

Mortification was the only word to describe how Ollie felt as she stood in the snow and buttoned her coat with quickly freezing fingers. Snowflakes fell on her bare head. Served her right. Her overreaction to Titus's gallant need to climb onto a roof for his boss meant she was nothing but a petty shrew.

However, she didn't know how to take back the words she said or how to deal with the roiling emotions in her chest. Could she blame the fact that the gifts, no, packages had thrown off her equilibrium, and she didn't want Titus to get hurt? Yet she had no right to expect Titus to listen to her. She wasn't his girl.

The door opened, and Titus emerged dressed in his winter coat, a hat in his hands, and a scarf over his arm. Without a word, he settled the hat over her hair, then wrapped the scarf around her neck, drawing her closer.

"Ollie." He held onto the ends of the scarf, keeping her in place. "Ollie, thank you for your concern. I'm sorry to have caused you to stress. It was not my intention whatsoever."

Ollie's jaw dropped open. He was apologizing for what *she* had done?

"I will admit I have been a coward." Titus adjusted his grip on the edges of the scarf. "In my desire to be a gentleman, I have not shown you my true motives. I have not wanted to hurt or cause you heartache, so I have remained quiet."

Ollie stared at him, unsure where he was going with any of this.

Titus looked down at his feet and then back at her. "I like you, Ollie. A lot. Do you think there's any chance ... could you possibly ... like me, too?" His cheeks turned red like a schoolboy's. "It's like we're back sharing our reading book. Even then, I had the silly idea to write down a question asking whether you might like me on that chalkboard. But the thought of you saying *no* … I could never get the nerve up to ask you. I haven't been brave enough until now, because seeing your concern for me made me realize that maybe I have a chance. I know this is the worst timing. I know you have this other man—"

Ollie stopped his words by placing her bare fingers over his mouth. Suddenly aware of the intimacy of the gesture, she yanked her hand away. Her words dried up. Her breathing increased.

Titus tugged on the scarf around her neck, urging her closer. "You don't have to answer me now. I just wanted you to know how I feel. And maybe, once this is over, we can talk about it again. Would that be okay?"

She looked up, determined to answer. He'd drawn her closer than she expected and her gaze stalled on his mouth, remembering how it had felt under her fingers. What would it feel like if he kissed her?

"Just nod," his voice cracked, "or shake your head."

She chuckled at the crack in his voice and it freed her from his spell. "I'd like that, Titus."

Hope lit his face and he leaned forward—to kiss her?

"Are we leaving yet?" Grandfather stomped out of the cabin, breaking the mood.

Ollie tried to jump away from Titus, but he held her within the circle of the scarf.

"I have my eye on you, Wilburn." Grandfather wagged a finger at Titus and Ollie wished she could melt into the snow. "I approved of your interest in my granddaughter but I'm also her chaperone. Now let's get a move on to the cabin and get this leak fixed. I have a neck to keep safe so you can call on my granddaughter."

Ollie turned back to Titus. "Grandfather approved?"

Titus grinned, fingers inching up the scarf. "You might say he gave me the kick in the hind end that I needed."

"Sounds like him."

"Mhmm. I shouldn't have let fear hold me back." Titus pressed a lingering kiss to her cheek. "But this is a promise that, with your permission, I won't let it any longer."

"Wilburn!" Grandfather bellowed.

Ollie and Titus laughed.

Ollie put a few things into her satchel, then they donned snowshoes. Titus wrapped her hand around his arm like a gentleman before traipsing through the woods to the cabin. Ollie was quite out of breath when they reached Casper's cabin. Titus set up the ladder, rested a board against the side of the house, and stuck a hammer in his belt. Ollie could scarcely breathe as Titus climbed the rungs, Grandfather standing underneath, anchoring the ladder. Ollie clasped her hands beneath her chin, praying to heaven for his safety.

Titus cleared the snow from the corner of the roof. "Yup, I see the problem. A shingle was blown loose, and there's a small puncture. A board will secure it for now, and then I can fix it once there's no snow. Ollie, can you hand me that piece there by the door?"

Ollie hefted the piece of wood Titus had prepared to cover the hole he expected to find, raising it above her head as he reached for it.

"Careful now," Grandfather muttered.

Titus stepped down a rung to reach the board better and his foot slipped. Ollie gasped. Titus, however, grabbed the board and secured himself back to the ladder. "I'm fine." He winked at her.

Ollie crossed her arms.

Titus climbed back up, hammered the board onto the roof, tucked the hammer back into his belt, and began to descend the ladder. He stepped carefully on the rung his foot had slipped on. His boot held steady, so he lowered his other foot to the next wrung. As his weight shifted, so did his other foot. It shot through the ladder, sending Titus backwards.

"Titus!" Ollie gasped.

"Whoa there!" Grandfather leaned back to hold the ladder steady.

Titus flailed, his grip coming up empty. Helpless, she watched him fall, one boot catching on a rung, jerking the ladder from Grandfather's grip. Titus landed flat on his back, the ladder on top of him.

Ollie ran to his side. He lay still, eyes closed, and she pressed a hand to his chest. It raised under her touch. "Titus? Titus, can you hear me?"

He didn't answer.

CHAPTER
SEVEN

Titus slowly became aware of the cold seeping into his body. His head throbbed as if someone had attempted to crack it open like an egg. *Egg*. The word reminded him of the danger facing Ollie, and he forced his eyes to open. Snowflakes fell on him as he squinted against the gray light.

"He's awake." Ollie's sweet voice came from his left.

He turned his head to find her despite the hammering between his temples. She smiled at him, looking oh so beautiful. Her stocking cap was covered in white flakes.

Her dark hair framed her face, and her nose was red from the chilly air.

"We were worried about you. You fell off a ladder. Remember?" A tear slid down her cheek. He reached up to swipe it away and gasped at the pain that shot through his body.

"At least your head's moving. Yer arm, too." Osborn's rough voice had Titus looking towards his other side. "Can you move your feet?"

Titus closed his eyes, unable to keep them open with the throbbing in his head and the shards of light in his eyes. However, he braced for the pain and raised his toes toward his shins, then shifted them from side to side.

"Good," Osborn said, and Ollie gave a grateful sigh. "You're not paralyzed."

That was a mercy, for sure. But gratefulness was challenging to come by when his body screamed in agony. He clenched his jaw, not wanting to show Ollie how much he hurt.

"That's the good news," Osborn continued. "That was some fall. Now we need to get you inside before you freeze. But I don't like movin' you."

"We need to go for a doctor," Ollie said. "I'll go into town—"

"No!" Osborn echoed Titus's emphatic word. Titus pried his eyes open so she could see his earnestness. "You can't, Ollie."

She touched his shoulder, and his concern for her was mirrored in her expression. "You need to see a doctor, Titus. Please."

"But you can't go into town." His voice quivered with the emotion cascading through him. Anger at his helplessness strengthened him enough to reach for her. "It's too dangerous, Ollie. I'll be fine."

She pressed his hand against her cheek. "How do you know you'll be okay unless you have a doctor to see you? You could have broken something, broken your back even. I can see how much it hurts you. And just because you can move your feet now doesn't mean that you will be able to move them tomorrow or the next day. I've read about cases like this. You could have a broken back and never walk again."

Titus walked his fingers around the back of her neck to draw her closer, her hair impeding his progress, and she seemed to pull further and further away from him. Or perhaps it was more like she shrank more and more inside herself. He fought the pain to raise himself enough to pull her toward him. "Ollie, I'm worried about you, too."

"I know." She unhooked his hand and held it close, allowing him to relax against the ground.

"Please don't go." He squeezed his eyes shut. "Hiding you up here was the point. I'll be fine after a little rest."

Osborn cleared his throat. "I'll go to town."

"What?" Titus gasped at the pain between his shoulders as he turned too quickly. He'd honestly forgotten the older man was still there.

"But you hate going to town," Ollie said.

Osborn grinned. "But I think this one will make a good grandson, and I'd like to keep him alive."

It was a good thing Titus's hand was where it was because, while Ollie let go, Titus caught her fingers in his, preventing her from scrambling away. "I would be honored to be your grandson, sir." And while he spoke to Osborn, he pinned his gaze on Ollie.

She sucked in a breath as she realized the implication of what he was saying, what he meant.

"Glad to hear that." Osborn patted his shoulder. "I aim to leave Ollie here in the cabin with you. Laying flat on your back like this, I trust you with my granddaughter. However, I also like knowing your intentions. If it gets out that I left the two of you alone, you'll have to make an honest woman of her."

"No." This time, Ollie managed to escape Titus's hold, and she scrambled to her feet. "I won't put Titus in that position. It's not fair."

Titus saw her fear and tried to reach for her, but he only groaned.

Ollie stamped her foot. "And you need to get into the house before you freeze or hurt your back worse than it is. How are we going to do that?"

He wouldn't let her push him away unless she wished him to leave her be. "Ollie, I'm not going anywhere until you answer my question."

Her jaw worked with silent emotion.

He fisted his hand as the pain kept him stuck, laying flat on his back when he wanted to hold her. "If you do not want to stay in the cabin, that is okay. The decision is yours. However, if you decide to stay, not only would I welcome your company, but I am perfectly alright with any potential consequences. As your grandfather said, my intentions are clear, but I won't corner you into a future together if that is not what you want."

Ollie stood still, like a rabbit that sensed danger. She studied him as a bird chirped overhead. Snow continued to fall. A shiver arched through Titus's body, sending pain spearing down his back and up through his head. He barely managed to contain a moan, but he did so because he wanted Ollie to decide based on what *she* wanted, not on his predicament.

Osborn huffed. "You two can finish this conversation after I head to town. Now, I'm getting another board, putting you on it, and dragging your sorry carcass inside."

With that, Osborn stomped away, leaving them alone. Titus closed his eyes, the darkness easing the sharp spike in his head.

"Titus?" Ollie whispered. "Are you serious about what you said? What you said earlier ... Do you like me ... like that?"

Titus forced his eyes open again to see her, and then he unfisted his hand, palm up on the snowy ground. "I like you, Ollie. I have ever since our teacher paired us together when we were school kids. However, I refuse to be like the person leaving you those packages. I would love to pursue a future with you, but I won't if that's not something you desire."

"I—"

"Before you answer, the question has become more complicated." He hated to add this, but he needed to be upfront about everything, even as fear tightened into a band around his chest. "I don't know what this fall will have done to me. What you said is true. There could be lasting consequences. It could affect my ability to provide, and my deputy position. Yes, right now, I can move my arms and legs, but there's no guarantee of tomorrow. There's no guarantee of how much damage was done."

"Oh, Titus." She dropped to her knees beside him, and he fought the urge to hide the tears that had to be shimmering in his eyes. "Your fall and any health problems that might lay ahead would have nothing to do with this."

"Then what is it? You can tell me."

Ollie folded her arms. "I don't want you to feel coerced into this. I've read too many books about conniving women to have any desire to be one of those."

Hope welled in his heart, and Titus wiggled his fingers, hoping Ollie would put hers within his clasp. "I feel anything but cornered, Ollie. I feel ... grateful."

"Here we go." Osborn returned. "Did I give you kids enough time to finish that conversation?"

"Grandfather." Ollie groaned but took Titus's hand.

Osborn gave a nod of approval. "Then let's get you moved."

Ollie squeezed, giving Titus the bolstering he needed to swallow back the pain as Osborn hefted him onto the board. Osborn dragged him inside as Ollie ran ahead in order to lay out a pallet before the stove.

Pain overwhelmed him, and he allowed darkness to take him.

Ollie stoked the stove and shifted the kettle to a front burner before returning to sit beside Titus's pallet. Her grandfather had been gone for a couple hours now, and with the heavy snowfall, might be unable to return with the doctor until well after dark.

Titus had been in and out of consciousness several times since Grandfather left. Whenever his eyes fluttered open, they revealed the pain that engulfed him. Ollie wished she had something to ease his discomfort, but Casper's cabin was empty of anything but the most basic of emergency supplies.

Grandfather had said it was probably the body's way of healing itself, and that she shouldn't worry. But how could she not? Watching helplessly was horrible. She also kept replaying the fact that he was more concerned about her and her feelings than he was about himself. Like a motion picture, she could see again his determination to forgo a physician's help just to keep her safe and it sparked something in her heart that she had never felt before, even with him.

Ollie adjusted the blankets, smoothing them around him just to give her hand something to do. She'd spent her time tidying up his cabin. She wanted him to wake to a warm and clean atmosphere.

Perhaps once the doctor arrived, they would be able to move him from the cold floor to his bed. Yes, it would be more awkward for her to care for him in the little side room than here in the main room, but if he would sacrifice for her, she could for him.

She pressed her cool hands to her cheeks. Even though nothing untoward was happening, this situation was entirely beyond her comfort.

The kettle whistled, so she poured herself a cup and settled in the rocker with *The Tale of Benjamin Bunny*, and read aloud. "One morning a little rabbit sat on a bank. He pricked his ears and listened to the trit-trot, trit-trot of a pony."

Titus shifted. Was her reading aloud waking him? Perhaps she should just read silently.

She made it through another page when Titus's voice brought her attention to him. "Why did you stop?"

"You need rest and I was afraid I woke you."

"Your voice is the best thing to wake me. Keep reading?"

How could she say no? So she backed up to the beginning again and told of Benjamin Bunny and the mischief that he and his cousin Peter got into in their attempt to rescue Peter's clothes.

"Now I know why I stopped reading once we finished school," Titus muttered as she closed the book. "Reading is not boring when you're the one doing it.

Ollie smoothed the illustrated jacket cover. "You flatter me."

Titus grumbled. "I'm in too much pain for such nonsense. I don't visit the library because I don't read. Do you have another of those little books? Your voice helps."

Here was something she could do for him. "I have Peter's tale. Would you like me to read that?"

Titus nodded then dropped his arm over his eyes with a groan.

"Is there anything else I can do?"

"Your voice is perfect."

And so she read and by the time she finished her tea, and raided Casper's bookshelf for Dickens's ghostly Christmas to read aloud, Titus was keeping his eyes open for much longer stretches.

"I'm glad to see more color in your face." Ollie tucked her books into her bag, then rose to replace *A Christmas Carol*.

"I would say I'm perfectly content down here, but it is dreadfully awkward lying flat on my back while you move around the cabin. I feel the most horrible host."

Ollie giggled, then mock glared at him. "You need to concentrate on getting better."

He held her gaze for an intense moment that pinned her in place by the bookcase, then blinked and asked. "Do you have my pistol?"

"Uhh." It took her a mental head shake to reorient herself. "Grandfather took off your holster before he left and set it on the table here. He didn't want you to be uncomfortable while you rested. Y-you don't think you need it, do you?"

"I would feel better having it close by." Titus faced the ceiling and closed his eyes. "Just in case."

Ollie shivered, but gingerly picked up the holster, with the pistol still inside. She hated guns and weapons of all kinds. Her hands shook as she stared at the worn leather that signified the tools of Titus's trade. He promised to protect her, protect their county. "Do you think that person will find me here?"

"Come here, Ollie. Please?" The concern in his voice prompted her to turn. Titus held out his hand to her, anguish on his face. "I can't get up to comfort you."

"Oh, Titus." Her hero. She brought the holster to him and set her hand in his. "You don't have to comfort me. You're in pain. I can see it."

Titus tucked their hands against his heart and closed his eyes again. "I was supposed to go back to town to be able to investigate the case. I'm afraid I'm going to have to leave that to Casper for now. So we might not get it solved as quickly. That leaves time for him to find you and I can't protect you if I can't sit up."

"Titus—"

"You were right, Ollie. I shouldn't have gotten on that ladder. The leak could have waited. I could have fixed the damage to the cabin, but I can't fix me. I'm sorry I let my pride get in the way. I'm sorry I didn't listen."

"Enough." Ollie used her free hand to turn his head so he would look at her. "You are my ..."

Her voice trailed off as words jumbled on her tongue. Her friend. Her Hero. Her ... True Love? Ollie's breath hitched.

"What am I to you, Ollie?"

She wasn't ready to say, so she bent over and placed a light kiss on his lips, then escaped to the other room.

CHAPTER EIGHT

Wednesday, December 17
8 days until Christmas

Titus refused to be tucked away in the side bedroom like a worthless bag of bones. Even if the doctor declared his bones were bruised and in need of significant healing. He wanted to be able to watch the front door, and, if he were entirely honest with himself, watch Ollie, too. So here he lay on his pallet beside the stove, propped up on pillows like some spoiled prince, and growing more irritable the higher the sun rose.

"Why don't you read to me as I chop these veggies?" Ollie raised a brow at him. She stood across the room at the table where she prepared their noon meal.

"I wish that'd be enough," Titus groused. If Ollie read, perhaps it would settle him, but his attempt at reading, especially when he wanted to impress her, would only make him angry. And wasn't that the crux of the matter? He wanted to show her he could protect her, provide for her, care for her.

"If you keep scowling like that, you'll scare all the dust bunnies away before I can sweep them."

"You swept them yesterday. I doubt they returned."

Her lips pressed together. He couldn't believe she'd kissed him yesterday. It had been the lightest, quickest kiss ... he almost wondered if he'd dreamt it. Only the distance she kept between them now told him he hadn't. If he didn't tread carefully, he could scare her away permanently. A thought that did not improve his mood.

"Fine." Ollie laid the knife on the table and dusted her hands, which appeared as orange as the carrot she was cutting. "Grandfather will return from his cabin soon and I'd like to have this on the stove. You can peel the potatoes."

Before he could agree—or disagree—Ollie had placed a pot on his left, a bowl of dirt-smudged potatoes on his right, and a towel on his lap.

"I'm sure you can wield a knife." She held out the handle of a small knife, a dare glimmering in her eyes.

He puffed his chest. "I can throw one just fine."

She snorted, and he grinned.

They worked in companionable silence as the bowl of potatoes gradually emptied beside him, and the angst seeped out of his body.

Before the doctor had returned to town at dawn this morning, he'd encouraged Titus to take medicine for the pain. But Titus refused because whatever the doctor had given him when he arrived last night had put Titus to sleep, only to wake unrested. Fortunately, the doctor also had willow bark, which Ollie made into tea. It was enough. Sort of. Not that he would admit otherwise.

At least the doctor didn't believe he broke anything and that, with plenty of rest, his body would make a full recovery in time. However, sitting still was not in Titus's nature.

Ollie cleared her throat and he realized his irritation had crept back in.

"I make a horrible patient," he sighed.

"I'm just glad to see your eyes looking clearer and the color back in your face." Ollie took the empty potato bowl back to the table as he peeled the last one. "Perhaps it would help you to think on the case. You might not be able to follow the clues, but the mystery author, Agatha Christie, has a sleuth named Hercule Poirot and he puts great stock in his little gray cells."

"We are taking detective advice from a novel?" He fought a grin as he watched her cheeks redden.

She raised her chin. "The Murder of Roger Ackroyd was a delightful read. We just got it in the library this fall. It was originally published in serial form for the *London Evening News*, but in '26, it was printed as a full book by the Collins Publishing House. It has quite the ending twist."

Titus let his grin loose. "Alright Detective Olivia Larson, let's talk over the case."

She took the kettle of potatoes and rinsed them in a bucket of water she'd had on the table. "Since it appears this person is following the pattern of the 12 Days of

Christmas, if we wait until those days are done, do you believe he will lose interest?"

Titus considered her question as he cleaned the knife with the edge of the towel before wrapping up the peelings. His conclusion sobered him. "If he's determined to have you, then I doubt he will stop until he's given you all twelve gifts." He tucked the knife under his pillow and patted the holster beside his pallet.

Ollie set the kettle on the stove. "I can't think of any library patrons who have made me uncomfortable. Does it have to be an unmarried man? All types visit the library."

Good question. Did this fit the hallmarks of an unhappily married man? He didn't think so, but he could see the worry settling in the stiff lines of Ollie's shoulders as she stoked the stove's fire. "How about, instead of guessing and causing you to question every person you meet, perhaps understanding the gifts would give us a better understanding of this person."

"I like that idea." Ollie gave the stew a stir.

"Grab yourself a blanket and sit down here by me." He gently arched his back to work out the stiffness, but pain shot through his neck. "Then tell me what you know about the song."

"Are you sure you don't want to be in ..." She flushed as she pointed to the side room. "It can't be comfortable down there."

"It's better than being alone." The honest statement jumped out before he could temper it.

Ollie wrapped a quilt over her shoulders and settled beside him. "I wish we could get the bed through the door. Maybe Grandfather can rig up some sort of cot. It's colder down here, which won't help your muscles relax."

This was the closest she'd been to him since "the kiss." Taking a chance, Titus wove their fingers together. She didn't flinch.

"The doctor doesn't want you walking for another couple days, but do you think sitting in the rocker would be okay?"

The thought of the hard chair made him wince. "I'll be fine, Ollie. Doc is sure I simply bruised my head and back."

"I heard him telling grandfather your back looked like an eggplant."

"A what?"

"Eggplant." She grinned, but it quickly faded. "He thought you were concussed, too. Should we talk about the case? Maybe those little gray cells need time to heal like your back does."

He squeezed her hand, and her mouth rounded as if she just now realized the connection. He rubbed his thumb over hers, hoping she wouldn't pull away, but determined to let her go if she wanted the distance.

She swallowed, still staring at their hands, but didn't move. "I know the poem 'The Twelve Days of Christmas' was put to the tune we know around the time I was born. But it's been a poem for much, much longer."

Titus sank into the pillows cushioning his sore back. It would be time for another dose of willow bark tea soon, but Ollie's voice, her closeness, were the best medicine. He had to get better soon so he could be the brawn to her beautifully brilliant brain.

Ollie wasn't sure quite why she hadn't immediately recognized when he'd taken her hand, but now she was keenly aware of it. She struggled to concentrate, mentally scanning the library shelves, looking for books on the 12 Days of Christmas, and whether any of those had been recently checked out.

As she roved the shelves, she continued to explain what she knew about the song and the poem. "I know the poem itself is over two hundred years old and has different variations, though no one quite knows the origin. Many believe it was possibly used as a catechism since the gifts correlate to tenets of Christianity."

"Like twelve gifts for twelve disciples?"

Ollie chuckled. "No. The twelve drummers drumming is likely representative of The Apostle's Creed. It's the eleven pipers piping that probably stands for the eleven faithful disciples ... twelve, minus Judas."

"Interesting." Titus stared at the ceiling, and she could almost hear the gears turning as he considered all she'd told him already. "What does partridge mean?"

"Likely Jesus crucified. Two doves are the two testaments. The three hens are faith, hope, love." Ollie shuddered. "It's creepy that he's using this song to base his gifts."

"You said there were other forms of it?"

"Yes. First of all, this person doesn't understand that the Twelve Days of Christmas actually begin on Christmas Day and end on Epiphany, in January."

"Really?" Titus's attention shot to her. "You're so smart. How could you ever—"

"Ever?" she prompted.

Titus turned away, but not before she saw the red creeping up his neck.

She took a guess. "Ever like ... like a man ... like you?"

He nodded.

When he didn't speak, she returned to the subject at hand. "The poem was originally published in a book called *Mirth Without Mischief* in the late 1700s, though it was much older ..."

"You thought of something." Titus's embarrassment had vanished. "Do you have that book in your library?"

"No, it's too old for our little library. But somebody asked me if I had it. They checked out a different book. Who was it?" Ollie huffed. "If I can remember the book, I'll remember the patron. If they haven't returned it, I could look over the checkout cards to see if the names would prompt a memory. I really need to go back to town."

"You know that isn't safe." Titus tightened his hold on her hand as if she'd run off. She had a habit of that.

"He hasn't physically threatened me." *Yet.*

Titus tucked their hands against his chest as he had done last night. "Right now, he is trying to win you over. But if he suffers from the delusion that I suspect he does, then if you decline his overtures, I worry that he will turn violent."

Ollie shifted closer. "But he wouldn't want to actually ... kill me, right? Because then I wouldn't be ..." She pressed her free hand against her stomach to hold down the nausea. Suddenly, the homey scent of stew didn't smell all that appetizing.

"Maybe my injury is a blessing." Titus's muttered words were like water on a fire.

"Why?"

"Because I would be holding you right now, and alone in a cabin is hard enough on your reputation. It's a good thing your grandfather is returning soon."

What was she supposed to say to that?

Titus laid his free arm over his forehead. "I don't enjoy reading the newspaper but it shows plenty of examples of the illogical things people do when they are obsessed.

I like being a small town deputy because the world can be such an evil place. I like helping widows and rescuing cats from trees, and keeping damsels in distress safe."

Ollie smiled, knowing he referred to her.

"I honestly don't like hunting criminals or figuring out how they think so I can track them down. There's a reason why Casper is the sheriff. When he brought in that outlaw two years ago, I'm the one who ... well, it was his life or mine. I've never forgotten that."

Her heart ached. " I'm sorry, Titus. I didn't realize you were the one ... that it happened to you. I thought it was Casper. I think everyone thinks it was Casper, and that's why he came up here to get away. Why would he leave you with the sheriff's role when you were probably hurting as much as he was?"

"Because he felt responsible." Titus's answer was swift. "Because he's the leader of our office. And because the woman he loved was injured when he failed to arrest the outlaw. During my year as sheriff, I had that weight on my shoulders. It is not me, Ollie. I am not cut out to take that kind of responsibility. I signed on as a deputy because I want to keep the peace. I want to make ladies like Mrs. Clark and Mrs. Holland smile. I want to fix roofs and help young ladies when they slip on a sheet of ice."

Ollie ducked at the memory.

"I'm not afraid to protect you. I will. You can count on it. But it's ... you. I have wanted to protect you since that day in the forest. Remember?"

Warming comfort washed through her. "You've always been my hero, Titus. I suppose that's what's made me so nervous around you. I've always seen you that way, and I didn't want to lose my hope with a dose of cold reality."

"You keep saying I'm a hero, but how can you see that as I lay here flat on my back?" Shuffling outside had Titus reaching for his gun. "Fine. At least I can shoot from down here if I have to."

"It's me!" A voice boomed from outside.

"It's Grandfather." Ollie pressed his arm to lower the pistol.

"He's not coerced?"

Ollie rolled her eyes.

Grandfather pushed inside, took in the scene, then slammed the door against the cold. "Ollie, you're staying here. He left a box of five rings on my porch this morning before I got there."

She watched the box drop from Grandfather's grasp to the table with a resounding thud that echoed through her body like an aftershock.

CHAPTER NINE

Thursday, December 18
7 days until Christmas

If Titus could've moved, he would have taken Ollie into town yesterday. However, as much as the pain had lessened, his movements were impossibly stiff. Still, he'd been slowly working on sitting up by himself this morning, much to Ollie's distress.

He forced himself to ignore her disgruntled expression as he lifted himself from his pallet of pillows.

His back ached, and he closed his eyes, breathing through the pain.

Titus wanted to be ready to move, and they would need to soon. It was only a matter of time before this person following Ollie found her here at Casper's cabin instead of her grandfather's. Osborn had to come and go, taking care of the animals at his place and Titus's horse, as well as providing a sense of security and propriety while Ollie stayed with Titus. Titus strongly believed it would be better to take Ollie back to town, and if he could walk, he would do just that.

As much as he wanted to flop back against the pillows, he slowly lowered himself as he released a controlled breath.

"I saw that grimace, Titus Wilburn," Ollie said from where she swept the floor near the front door. "Stop torturing yourself."

Titus kept his eyes closed as he willed his back to relax. He had to face facts. Since sitting up was the extent of his ability, he would need to send Osborn back to town to get Casper. Or the new deputy.

Last night, Osborn had said he met the new man, Gideon Lundgren: a young, serious gent, of whom

Osborn approved. That was all the recommendation Titus needed. Apparently, Lundgren didn't live in their county but was looking for work to support his recently widowed mother and siblings, much like Eira Mae had done. Another point in the new deputy's favor.

Titus hoped Casper would send Lundgren as backup to protect them here at the cabin. He hated letting Ollie out of sight, but he had to be honest with himself. He couldn't protect her as she needed, so he'd have to sacrifice his pride to keep her safe.

"That is a heavy sigh." Ollie's voice had moved much closer, though Titus hadn't heard her steps.

He opened his eyes to find her looking down at him with concern.

"We need help, Ollie. I need to send a message to Casper."

She lowered herself beside him on the pallet and touched his arm. "It's okay to need help, Titus."

He clenched his jaw against the words that wanted to pop out, that he was supposed to be her protector. That he'd let his stupidity put her in danger. Some hero he was.

"I found a copy of *Treasure Island* on Casper's bookshelf. I'll read that aloud. It has enough adventure to distract you until Grandfather returns from morning chores."

Bless Ollie for trying, but even her beautiful voice couldn't capture his concentration. His ears kept straining for any movement outside. He kept checking and rechecking his weapon, then ensuring himself that the knife still lay under his pillows. Not that he could twist around to grab it easily. *What were you thinking?* Getting on the roof when Ollie's safety was at risk.

"I see you're agitated again." Ollie looked over the book at him.

If it weren't for the danger, this would be a moment he'd forever capture in his memories. The girl he'd loved for years tending his injuries, reading to him, looking so content as she gently rocked in the rocking chair before the stove. He could see them together decades from now. "I must find a way to protect you while I am stuck here."

The book dropped to her lap. "We have been over this already, Titus. I don't think less of you because you are injured."

"I'm grateful for that, but it doesn't change the situation." Titus shifted against the pillows. The bruises were beginning to itch. "The rings in yesterday's box prove you are still in danger, and I think the best way is to have someone else protect you. I can't."

"No!" Ollie slapped the book on the little table beside the rocker, rattling the glass chimney of the lamp. "I don't want anyone else to protect me. I trust you. I'm like my grandfather, I prefer to keep to myself. That's why the library suits me. It's quiet. Patrons visit, so I see people, but they don't stay long, and if they do talk, it's about a book. And I can talk about a book. But having to rely on another man? Be stuck in a cabin like this with someone else? Even if that someone else is Casper. Please don't do that to me, Titus. I can't. I can't."

"Okay, okay." Titus eased himself to a sitting position, wishing to jump to her side to comfort her. Witnessing her like this, hearing the panic in her voice, had Titus seeing her in a new light. He gentled his tone. "Ollie, once again, you have surprised me. You have more layers than I ever dreamed of. And I have known you most of our lives."

Her cheeks bloomed a beautiful pink, encouraging him to continue.

"You know I like exploring. And getting to know you better. Friendship is nice, but …" Dare he? Yes, yes, he did. "But I like the idea of more."

Her eyes widened like twin moons. Wonder and fear and hope swirling in their depths.

His back would give out soon, but he couldn't say this while lying down. He braced his hands behind him. "I've enjoyed my time with you for years, Ollie. I simply haven't been brave enough to risk our friendship. But it's not enough for me anymore. I want a lifetime to learn everything there is about you. To hear all the things you want to say. Listen to your voice as you read—" Titus's back spasmed, and he groaned as he collapsed onto his back.

In an instant, Ollie was at his side, a tear on her cheek. "Please stop hurting yourself. I hate seeing you in pain."

He gritted his teeth to raise his hand to her face.

"Is there anything I can do?" She captured his fingers before they could reach her and held them under her chin. While she hadn't acknowledged his declaration with words, he felt her agreement deeply within his heart. Instead of running away, as she usually did, she drew near.

They had to find a way to get this person to leave her alone, or she would look over her shoulder her whole life. "Can you find the Twelve Days poem and read it to me?"

She shook her head, and her body relaxed. "You're determined, aren't you? All right. Today is day six, six geese a-laying. I do hope he won't harm any."

"He didn't hurt the doves or the hens." Titus hoped to ease her worry.

"True, and he didn't harm the pheasant out of cruelty exactly, but because he wanted to make me a meal. But something is disturbing about that, regardless. Why send me that and not ... cook it first?"

"I don't think we can truly understand because I don't think he's thinking logically." Whether it was her touch or the calm reminder of what they were up against, Titus felt as if he could breathe for the first time since he awoke that morning. "Let's send your grandfather to talk to Casper, and we'll make a plan from there."

"As long as I can stay with you, I'll do whatever you think is best."

Titus's chest expanded at the confidence she placed in him, and the hope of a future together.

Later that afternoon, as the sky began to darken, Ollie found herself pacing the cabin while Titus napped. He wouldn't admit how much pain he was still in, and he too often wore himself out trying to push himself to recover. Much to her consternation, he'd convinced Grandfather to help him stand before the older man left for town. While she hated the pain it caused, seeing Titus standing on his own was also a great relief.

The kettle whistled, and she poured the hot water into a teapot. This waiting for something to happen had her on edge. She kept wanting to open the door to see what was happening beyond the walls of this cozy cabin, yet feared what she would find. Another package on the doorstep? The man who insisted that she was his true love?

She spooned peppermint tea leaves into the teapot to steep. Her mama had always sworn peppermint could ease any worry. As she'd reminded Titus earlier, today was day six of this horror story, which meant the man would try to send her six geese a-laying. He'd already given her eggs for the three French hens, so what would he give her today? Would he leave the gift at Grandfather's cabin or try to find her?

Ollie let the tea steep as she continued pacing. She feared with each animal gift, it would be another dead bird—or whatever number he was on—which would be even worse. Yet, as she pointed out, the man hadn't repeated that first offense.

The thought had been needling her for days now, and having said it aloud this morning, it had nestled into her head. He could have actually given her two dead doves or three dead hens and could still leave her six dead geese ... so why hadn't he?

She paused in her pacing, the thought hitting her.

"Ollie, what is it?" Titus asked from his pallet on the floor beside the stove. How long had he been awake? "Ollie?"

She poured herself a cup of tea, or tried to. Her hands shook so that she spilled more than she should have. "I-I think he watched me—us—that first day."

Instead of dismissing her, Titus hummed in agreement. "He would have seen your reaction to the dead bird."

Ollie left the cup on the sideboard beside the stove, not wanting to risk dropping the steaming liquid. "He hasn't given me another one."

"Well, besides the incredibly creepy feeling of having someone watching you, I hate to admit it shows a shred of compassion."

She wrapped her arms around herself as a shiver raced through her. "But it's even creepier then because he's trying so hard. Oh, why did he have to pick me?"

"Because you're sweet and kind. Why wouldn't he fall in love with you?"

Ollie spun to face him as she realized what he had said. The light in his eyes confirmed he wasn't talking about the man leaving her gifts. She hadn't known how to respond to his declaration earlier. Her heart had filled with the desire to care for him in any way she could, but, like now, no words formed on her tongue.

A noise sounded outside before either of them could comment on her silence.

Titus pushed to a seated position, left hand braced behind him, right grasping his pistol. "It's too early for your grandfather to have returned, and I'm not expecting Casper. Though it could be him, I suppose. Just stay over there behind the door." Titus motioned to where she should stand. His jaw tensed, and Ollie could see how much physical pain this caused him. He cocked the hammer of the pistol and called out to the person at the door.

No answer came, nor did any sound. An animal would have fled, making scrambling noises, and one glance at Titus's expression told Ollie that her gifter had found her. Titus pressed his finger to his lips, then pointed to the door with a motion to open it.

Her body trembled, but Titus gave her a nod. She opened the door slowly at first, then yanked it toward her, hiding behind while Titus faced the threat.

"This is Deputy Titus Wilborn. Identify yourself."

No response.

"I'm armed and will ..."

A long shadow stretched into the cabin. "I know she's here. I know you're trying to ruin my girl."

Ollie willed her knees not to buckle.

"Have you asked her whether she is your girl?" Titus asked, surprisingly calm. And it terrified her because she remembered what he'd had to do once before. And now he aimed a gun at another man, knowing he might have to kill or be killed once again.

"Olivia Larson is my true love." The man had moved into the room enough that she could see his black coat and the rifle muzzle sticking out beside his leg, where Titus couldn't see it. "And you can't have her."

The man raised the rifle. *No!* Ollie pushed the door, slamming it into his arm, throwing off the rifle blast. Ollie's ears rang, and she stumbled, clinging to the door to keep from falling. Titus fired his weapon. The other man yelped and high-tailed it out the door. Ollie slammed it shut, then pulled the table to hold it closed.

Breathing heavily, she leaned against it and stared at Titus, who stared right back. What else was there to say when there, between them, were six goose feathers?

CHAPTER TEN

Friday, December 19
6 days until Christmas

"Casper's right." Titus leaned against the kitchen table, which rested against the door where it had sat since Ollie had moved it there the day before. No matter how much his back screamed at him, this was not a conversation he could have lying on that dratted pallet. Not when Ollie, Casper, and Osborn all stared at him.

"I'm not leaving you here by yourself." Ollie crossed her arms, standing both fierce and forlorn. "The man shot at you, not me. He wants me to be his … You're the one who's actually in danger."

"She's right." Casper rested his hands on his holster belt. "Both of you need to come back to town. We'll arrange—"

"I can't." As much as Titus wanted to walk out of there, simply standing, no, simply *leaning* against this table was taking all of his mental energy. Getting on a horse would be excruciating, and a wagon couldn't make it up to the cabin.

Osborn grunted and settled into the rocker.

"Well, this tells me that priority number one next summer is widening the road so we can get some type of wheeled conveyance up here." Casper jerked a kitchen chair around to sit and lean his arms on the back. "There were too many library records for me to bring here, but since Eira Mae is not allowed to do much other than sit down, I set her to the task of sorting through the records as you suggested, Ollie."

"I hate to take her from Lewis." Ollie paced.

"Don't worry. My aunt is watching Lewis." Casper turned his intense gaze on Titus, underscoring why Titus believed the man embodied a sheriff. "I'm going to find this man. Toying with Ollie was bad enough, but attempting to murder one of my deputies? Not on my watch."

Titus swallowed, both amazed and humbled by the loyalty of his friend and boss.

"That's all well and good," Osborn broke in, "but what do you know of this man to be able to track him? He snuck around and followed Ollie without anyone being the wiser."

Ollie shuddered. Thankfully, Casper toed a chair toward her. Titus would have insisted, but he couldn't move from the table without help.

"From my experience, I can tell a few things." Casper ticked them off on his fingers. "First, we know full well he is here somewhere. Two, that tells me he knows how to handle the forest in the winter. Which means, three, he's likely from around here."

Osborn huffed. "He ain't from these woods, so he's hiding somewhere you can find. While you search, you can count on me to protect these two. My rifle still aims true."

"Grandfather!"

"Osborn." Casper glared at him. "We don't shoot first."

Osborn grunted. "Who said anything about shooting the man? I was a crack shot in the war, I don't actually have to put a hole in him."

Ollie dropped her head into her hands. Titus ducked his head to hide a smile.

"I did my time during the war," Osborn continued. "I swore I would never shoot another human being, and I don't plan to go back on that promise. But if the life of my granddaughter and her—what are you to her now, Wilburn? Can I call a preacher yet?"

"Matching making, are you Osborn?" Casper chuckled.

"Got any objections, Sheriff?" Osborn demanded.

"Not a one." Casper grinned. "I've been waiting for this one to speak his mind long enough."

"We are right here," Titus growled. Poor Ollie's face was as red as a holly berry. "Cas, just deputize Osborn so that if he does have to shoot someone, it's official."

"I don't need no pay or anything," Osborn said. "And I'll hand the whole deputy thing right back to you once this is over. I ain't interested in anything but my granddaughter's well-being. When this is over, I want to go back to my cabin where everyone has to leave me alone until these two bring me great-grandchildren."

Ollie squeaked.

"What?" Osborn winked at Titus. "I want great-grandchildren before I die, so hurry up."

"Back to the actual situation here," Titus ground out. He needed to end this conversation before Ollie ran away or his back stopped holding him up—and at the rate things were going, he wasn't sure which would happen first.

Casper sighed. "You say you didn't recognize the man?"

Titus shook his head. "Never seen him before, which tells me he's not someone we've had at the jail."

"Ollie?"

She kept her chin down. "I-I didn't see him, but from the way Titus described him and the duster coat he wore, I-I have a suspicion."

"Go on." Casper pinned her with one of his intense stares.

Titus's grip on the table tightened, but he shut his mouth. He had to let Casper be sheriff, even if he wanted to defend Ollie.

Ollie hugged herself. "I won't give a name without proof."

Osborn grunted again, but Titus found himself smiling. That was his girl. *His girl?*

Casper, however, didn't relent. "That doesn't help keep Titus safe."

"Hey." Titus pushed off the table to defend Ollie, but one step without support, and his body gave out. He crashed to the ground, pain robbing him of all his senses.

"Titus!" Ollie's voice cut through the rushing in his ears.

"Don't move. We got you." Casper.

Then, jostling and pain and a cool hand on his forehead. "You're back on the pallet, Titus. Let your back relax. I'll get you some willow bark tea."

"Don't." He tried to reach for her.

She squeezed his fingers. "I'm not going anywhere, but you need medicine."

Not as much as he needed Ollie. He refused to let go of her and instead pried his eyes open to find Casper. "We can't leave the cabin, so who can you send to guard it?"

Casper raised a brow. "Let's start by not opening the door so that he can just walk inside."

Pain ignited his anger at Casper's prod. "It was the best I could do from down here. I had Ollie safe."

"You shot your weapon in her direction."

"No." Titus jabbed his free hand at a spot above the door. "I owe you a patch job. Didn't hit him. Didn't aim at him. Simply fired to make him think I was."

Three sets of eyes looked at him, all registering their approval and respect.

Titus tucked his chin, thumb rubbing Ollie's knuckles. "I wouldn't endanger Ollie. I love her too much."

Perhaps he should have saved his declaration for later, but it was too important. He had nothing to hide from his boss or her grandfather. Osborn had the right of it. Titus would marry her tonight, tomorrow ... He'd marry her in a year or whenever she thought it best. And if it would protect her, he'd marry her in an hour, as long as they could spend the rest of their lives together.

Ollie was all jumbled up, so as soon as she saw Titus resting comfortably after drinking the willow bark tea, she escaped to the bedroom to catch her breath. She should make supper. At this point, she'd clean the house again or even organize the bookshelves—anything to keep her hands busy as she tried to wrestle her thoughts into some type of order.

Titus had declared his love.

Giddy, warm, wonderful feelings filled her. And she didn't miss that he made such a declaration in front of her grandfather and Casper.

Did she say something? Acknowledge that he loved her?

Ollie plopped onto the bed in defeat. No. She did not. For a girl who loved words, who loved books, who rambled copious words when she was nervous, those very words had failed her. Twice.

Then there was the man leaving her gifts.

Ollie dropped her face into her hands. She was confident the man had shot at Titus because Titus loved her. Somehow, the man had figured it out and decided to take action, something Ollie couldn't even do. It also confirmed to her that the man was watching her.

Was she right in her suspicions? If she was, she felt horrible for the awkward young man. He'd been nothing but kind, visiting the library and asking for books to read. He lived in a small cabin outside of town. An only child whose mother died when he was small, he lived there with his father, whom Ollie was sure treated him poorly. She'd witnessed other youths doing similarly, since Seth was slower at most things.

She never would have suspected him except that he always wore that black coat. Given a clearer mind, she recognized the worn spot on his elbow. He always rested it on her counter when he came to ask for a book. Usually, it was a children's book with lots of pictures since his father had taken him out of school before he learned to read.

Ollie rubbed her temple. This was the most awkward, horrible love triangle she could imagine. It wasn't a triangle, not really, but Seth—or someone who wanted her to think it was Seth—thought it was, and that person was trying to eliminate the competition. Would it be better for her to get distance from Titus? Perhaps, but she understood Titus's perspective too well: that by being close to her, he could keep her safe, even if he thought himself an unlikely hero.

"Ollie?" Casper knocked at the door.

She didn't want to talk, not yet.

"Titus is worried about you." The censure in his tone told her he would side with his friend on this. "Join us out here."

She pushed cheer into her voice and spoke loud enough for Titus to hear her. "Be there in a moment." Because she would side with Titus, too.

Ollie turned the doorknob but didn't open it. If her gift-giver were Seth, he wouldn't harm her. If she stayed close, then, she could protect Titus. Seth would listen to her, too. And if not, she wouldn't hesitate to offer herself in exchange for Titus's life. Titus wouldn't understand, or maybe he would since he would do the same. She didn't doubt that he would step in front of a bullet for her.

She leaned on the door jamb. The trouble was that she couldn't believe Seth was the one behind this. Perhaps he'd leave her the gifts in his child-like way, even watch her from a distance. But he would never harm her, would never shoot at Titus. No. Ever-kind Seth would never do something like that. He did not have a mean bone in his large body. That's why she wouldn't give Casper his name.

"Ollie?" Casper knocked again. "Do I send in your grandfather?"

She yanked the door open, throwing Casper off balance. "Can't a lady fix her hair without getting yelled at?"

Casper had the decency to rub his reddening neck. Instead of replying, he jabbed his chin at Titus's pallet, which was empty.

"Where is he?" She scanned the small space and instantly spotted him leaning heavily on a long pole someone must have fashioned into a walking stick for him. Grandfather hovering. *Oh, Titus.*

"I can't talk sense into him." Casper planted hands on his holster belt. "He's determined to protect you and hates being laid up on the pallet."

"He's going to hurt himself worse if he doesn't allow his back to heal."

"You tell him that. He won't hear it from me."

Ollie nodded, realizing this was one of the longest, non-stuttering conversations she'd had with the sheriff. It gave her the courage to add, "I have a name for you, but I need you to promise me something before I tell you."

Titus saw her then and immediately ducked his chin like a boy caught reading a book with sticky hands. Grandfather laughed.

"Who are you protecting, Ollie?" Casper watched Titus work his way toward them, Grandfather still at his side.

Tears pricked her eyes. "It's not who I think, but someone wants me to think it is."

Who would want people to believe that Seth was a danger? Would they go so far as to set him up by killing Titus? Perhaps Seth began this ill-fated gift-giving, but he was not the man who showed up at the cabin yesterday. And while she had no reason to think her gift-giver would want to kill her, she did believe he wouldn't hesitate to remove Titus from her life. And she would do everything in her power to make sure that didn't happen.

"Ollie." Casper's warning was low enough for Titus not to hear, but Titus scowled.

"You were going to rest."

Titus ignored his boss and focused on her.

"I turn my back, and you're up again." Ollie handed Casper the stick so she could tuck her hand around Titus's arm. "You need to rest. We've talked about this."

"You tell him, girlie," Grandfather muttered.

"Ollie." Casper stabbed the stick into the ground, drawing everyone's attention. "Who do you think shot at my deputy?"

"Leave her alone, Cas." Titus straightened despite the grimace.

"No." Casper folded his arms, looking big and intimidating. Ollie tucked herself closer to Titus. "There is someone dangerous out there, and I want to find him."

The truth of that statement set Ollie trembling.

Suddenly, a great squawking erupted outside. Casper shoved Ollie and Titus into the bedroom, causing Titus to nearly bring Ollie down when he leaned all his weight on her shoulder. Grandfather caught Titus under the other arm, unceremoniously dumped him on the bed, then shouldered his rifle and slammed the door behind him.

Titus groaned as he lay on the bed. Ollie spun in a circle, unsure how to help. She heard the front door open, and Titus shifted with a moan. His face was ashen, but he held his pistol.

Propriety couldn't stand in a moment like this, so she tucked herself under his left arm to allow him to sit up. He leaned heavily on her, holding her as he braced his shooting arm on his bent knee.

"Who ... who is being set up?" The words cost Titus energy he couldn't spare, so she didn't hesitate to answer. His jaw tightened at Seth's name. "I know Seth. He wasn't the shooter. He wouldn't do this."

Squawks grew louder. "Someone wants us to think it's him."

"Easy to blame a kid people think is slow." Titus's nose flared. "They don't see his kindness."

Grandfather hollered something incoherent.

Titus turned to her at the same time she looked at him. An inch apart, they spoke at the same time. "Seven swans a-swimming."

"Stay with them, I'm going after him," Casper shouted.

Grandfather hauled open the bedroom door. "He just sent seven swans into the room. He's trying to flush you out."

CHAPTER ELEVEN

Saturday, December 20
5 days until Christmas

Ollie startled as the mantle clock struck midnight, then again when Casper opened the front door.

"No sign of him." Casper shrugged out of his coat. "Vanished into the forest."

"I should have gone after him instead." Grandfather adjusted his grip on the rifle he'd kept on his knees all night.

Ollie busied herself at the stove where the coffee kettle simmered. Titus had fallen asleep on the bed once the swans had been removed from the house, so she'd left him to sleep and joined her grandfather in the main room. She couldn't help jumping at every noise, but all had remained eerily quiet.

"Where's Titus?" Casper dropped into the straight back chair across from Grandfather.

"Finally resting." Grandfather sipped his coffee.

Ollie brought Casper a cup, which he took with a grateful smile. She stood between the two men, worrying her hands. Was she brave enough to share the idea that had been growing into plan?

"Spit it out," Grandfather grunted.

Casper raised his brows.

"I have an idea I don't think you'll like." She wished Titus were awake, though he would probably not like this idea any more than her grandfather and Casper would.

Casper used his foot to push a chair in her direction. "Sit down and spell it out. We can't see whether it has merit unless you tell us."

She sat and stared at her hands, knowing if she looked at either her grandfather or Casper, she would lose her nerve. "I-I think … I think I know who l-left the first gift. Perhaps even the second and third. Not this one, not the swans. I-I can't fathom who would have s-swans. It's winter. But if I talk to him, perhaps I can get an understanding of what's going on?"

"You aren't leaving this cabin." Casper crossed his arms.

"Can you bring the person here?" Grandfather leaned back in his chair.

Ollie nodded. "I think that would be the wisest choice. But Casper, you have to promise me that you won't hurt him. Please, please don't scare him or blame him for any of this. It's not him. Titus agrees. He's being set up, too. Whoever it is, he's using him because he's —

"You're talking about Seth." Casper's arms dropped to the table. "I agree entirely. Seth would not send swans in here and would never shoot at Titus. He and Titus get along. In fact, whenever I need to intervene because

Seth took something without realizing he had to pay for it, I always send Titus to take care of him. It's not Seth."

"But you think this Seth could be behind the gifts?" Grandfather asked.

Again, Ollie nodded. "He is so kind and sweet that it wouldn't surprise me if he tried to offer a gift like an uncooked pheasant. He probably thought he was giving me Christmas dinner. Perhaps he heard the song, and it gave him the idea. He probably found the dove figurine and wanted to give it to me as a Christmas gift. I-I hate that he might have seen my terrified reaction to the pheasant because that would have hurt him. But he doesn't have a jealous bone, so there would be no reason for him to hurt Titus."

"I agree." Casper's simple statement washed a wave of relief, followed by exhaustion, over her. Suddenly, she felt as if she hadn't slept in days.

"Will he agree to come to the cabin?" Grandfather asked. Ollie closed her eyes, listening to the clock tick its way toward the next hour.

"If I leave now, I can return before the suspect regroups. Osborn, will you be alright protecting them without me? If Seth holds an answer, I think both Ollie and Titus need to talk with him.

"And Titus can't leave this cabin." Grandfather's statement brought her attention to him. "He needs to rest his back, or he's never going to walk again."

Weariness fled in the face of fear. "Do you really think that?"

"I'm sorry, girlie, but I do. You heard the doctor say that based on the symptoms, Titus bruised, if not broke, his back. Too many fellow soldiers tried to walk too early. It's just going to aggravate his back or, worse, cause further damage."

Ollie rubbed her eyes. "I wish I had my books to research it more."

"Take my experience, then. Titus needs to rest, not walk."

"As long as I don't have to stay in that room, I'll sit all the live-long day." Titus appeared in the bedroom doorway, leaning on the stick he'd used earlier. "I know I've been pushing myself too hard, but your safety matters too much to me, Ollie. But Osborn is also right. I can't think only of this moment, I have to think of the future, too. What kind of life can I offer you if I can't walk?"

Ollie crossed the room to tuck herself under his free arm, her heart hammering as she absorbed his declaration. She helped him to the rocking chair and adjusted the pillows for his comfort. He sat, looking up at her with eyes full of love for her, and she finally knew exactly what to say. "Titus, no matter what happens, whether you can walk fine or never will, whether you have a job or not ... Where you go, I will go. It's as simple as that."

"Ollie." A tear escaped down his cheek.

Grandfather grunted. "Bring the preacher with you, Yarwood. These two are spending the rest of Christmas here, and I want them married so I don't have to chaperone them."

Ollie felt heat bloom in her cheeks. Casper gave a nod, but looked to Titus for approval. Titus captured Ollie's hand. "Will you marry me, Ollie?"

The choice was hers. "Yes, Titus. I can think of nothing better than a lifetime with my best friend."

If it wasn't for the pain in his back, Titus would be confident he was dreaming. Near his feet, Ollie lay asleep on the pallet Titus had used the last couple of days. Her hair fanned out around her beautiful face.

He'd refused to lie down, content to rest in the rocker because he wanted to be ready if anything happened while Casper was gone. Osborn, his future grandfather-in-law, cleaned his rifle at the kitchen table as dawn began filtering into the room. Nervous excitement pulsed through Titus. By tonight, they should know who had been harassing Ollie and, best of all, Ollie would be his wife. If Seth had put this whole situation into motion, Titus might have to thank him. Without that pheasant, would he and Ollie have ever broken through their hesitation to see their friendship as more?

Rustling outside drew his attention. Osborn snapped his rifle into position. Titus gripped his pistol. If it was Casper, he would give a holler. The fact that no greeting came meant the man after Ollie had returned. Titus nudged her foot and she blinked awake. He put his finger to his lips and nodded for her to go into the side bedroom, but she shook her head.

"I'm staying by you," she whispered as she shifted to her knees.

Her hair cascaded down her shoulders, and for a moment, he was dumbstruck. A bump outside yanked him back to reality, and he waved her near. She tucked herself between the rocker and the stove, the perfect little protective spot that put him between her and the door. Another reason he loved her. She was brave in standing beside him yet depended on him to be her hero. His shoulders went back as he braced for what—or who—would come through the door.

A tin clanked, and then a white substance slowly trickled under the crack between the door and floor. It soaked into the wood boards before Titus could quite believe what he was seeing. More clanking, then more white seeped under the door.

"Is that milk?" Osborn mumbled.

"Eight maids a-milking," Ollie muttered beside him.

Titus allowed himself two deep breaths to steady the emotions swirling inside. Anger, frustration, concern, bewilderment. None of that would help him in the next few minutes.

Ollie held up three fingers, then four, and he realized she was counting each pail. Did he confront the man before he poured all eight? This wasn't time for waiting.

Titus cocked the hammer, Osborn following suit. Titus listened for the fifth clink, then called, "If you're looking for Ollie, she's taken."

"Titus, don't." Ollie gripped his knee.

The sixth pail of milk pooled into the cabin.

As much as Titus wanted to goad the man into answering, he kept his tone conversational, questioning. "Why do you insist on making Ollie your true love?"

Ollie's fingers shook as she held up seven. Osborn glanced over, silently asking for the plan. But Titus didn't have one. Last time they opened the door, the man shot at him. Titus didn't want to shoot him any more than Osborn did. They simply wanted the man to leave Ollie alone. Conversation hadn't worked either. So what would?

The eighth pail of milk slowly seeped into the room, swirling with another smell he hadn't expected. Kerosene.

Osborn jumped out of his chair as the clear liquid spread atop the spilled milk. One match and the oil would ignite, sending the door—and the only way out of the cabin—into flames.

Before Titus could convince his back to let him stand, Ollie darted for the door and flung it open. "Don't hurt them."

Osborn froze at the pistol pointed his way by the masked man who had snaked his arm around Ollie's shoulders. Ollie's gaze pinned Titus to his rocker. He knew what she was doing, would have done the same.

"L-leave them be," Ollie's voice wobbled, "and I-I will go peacefully."

Titus's heart fractured. "Ollie, no."

The mask failed to hide the triumphant gleam in the man's eyes before he slammed the door shut. Titus snatched the walking stick and charged for the door as Osborn flung it open. But Ollie had vanished into the trees with her abductor.

Titus slammed his hand against the door jamb, the motion knocking him off balance. His foot slipped on the mix of milk and kerosene and he landed in a heap at Osborn's feet.

"Go after her." Titus snapped as pain lanced through his back. "I can't lose her."

"Can you manage?" Osborn hesitated.

Titus willed away the emotion clogging his throat. "She'll marry him if it will save me. I can't let her, but I can't do anything about it. You have to rescue her."

"Send Casper after my trail as soon as he arrives." Osborn stepped into the snow.

Titus bowed his head, prayer the only tool he could wield.

CHAPTER TWELVE

Sunday, December 21
4 days until Christmas

Ollie shivered in the cold, snow-encased hollow, wishing she was back with Titus in Casper's cabin, knowing that her sacrifice had kept him and Grandfather alive. Had her abductor lit the kerosene, she had no doubt the man would have shot Titus as soon as he escaped the burning cabin.

She burrowed deeper under the pelts he had left for her, using her chin to inch them toward her nose. Her arms and legs were trussed up behind her like a Christmas turkey. For the past twenty-four hours—she guessed it'd been that long, but didn't know for sure—she made herself recite her blessings. Like having not frozen to death overnight.

Her abductor, who had been wearing a mask, had left her tied in this secluded spot as soon as they'd arrived. She hoped that would give her grandfather a chance to rescue her—Grandfather was an expert tracker—but hope waned as the day wore on. Then fear set in. Had he harmed her grandfather to keep him from finding her?

As the snow had begun to fall and the wind picked up, fear had threatened to turn to panic. She tried to be thankful for the packed snow and deep brush that protected her as the weather turned into a full blizzard, but bound and defenseless, she could only hope an animal wouldn't seek out this tiny refuge.

It was now Sunday, and the snow had tapered. She should be thankful for such a short storm, grateful that she hadn't been trapped with the man as the wind howled. Yet tears clogged her nose. With so little daylight, could Grandfather find her? Was Titus still alive, and was there a way to get out of this so she could return to him? They were going to be married last night. Instead, she had spent the night alone.

And survived.

Thank you.

How had Titus spent the night? Terrified for her, no doubt. The storm would have kept them from searching for her and erased all the tracks left behind. Had Casper returned to the cabin before the storm hit? Did he find Seth? Were Eira Mae, Lewis, and her unborn baby all right if Casper had been trapped at the cabin?

Ollie's heartbeat picked up speed, and she twisted her raw wrists in another futile attempt to get free. What if her abductor forgot where he left her? She couldn't get free. She was stuck here at the mercy of the wind and the cold and the animals.

How she wished for Titus.

Weak light filtered through the snowy limbs outside the snow hollow. The blizzard hadn't penetrated this dense area of forest as much as she suspected it had in other areas. Would Titus and grandfather even be able to get out of the cabin? She'd been in blizzards before where the snow had piled against the door, leaving no way out. *Be thankful.* It had been a short storm. Fierce, but it had quickly moved on.

The crunch of boots tore her from the maelstrom of worry. Was it Titus or was it her kidnapper? A shadowy form ducked under the low branches and crawled into the hollow.

"Hello, Olivia."

Ollie gapped. "Mr. Anderson?" Seth's father?

"I'm afraid I can't wait for Christmas Eve for us to be married, so we shall have the ceremony tonight." He tucked a strand of her hair behind her ear.

She recoiled. "What are you doing?"

The man reared back. "I need a mother for the brat and a replacement for the woman who bore him."

"What?" Her cold, tired mind scrambled to keep up. "Seth is nearly an adult. You could marry any woman. W-why me?"

"You're pretty enough. Quiet, too. I need quiet." Anderson shrugged as if choosing what to order at the diner. "Seth likes you, so you'll be able to keep him out of my way."

"I've barely talked with you. I hardly know you." She scarcely recognized him. Since last she'd seen him with Seth, he'd shaved his beard and trimmed his hair. The man looked as if he were ready to court someone. Nausea swam in Ollie's stomach. He wanted to court *her*.

"Oh, don't be coy. I've seen how you look at me. You have been dying for me to ask you to marry me. Of course, that deputy knew just how to turn your head, empty as it is. I should have intervened as soon as Seth left you that bird. Stupid boy. I'm sure the storm brought you to your senses. Let's get to the chapel."

"No." Ollie shied away from him until she was tucked against the snow-encased branches that made the back of the hollow. "I don't want to marry you."

Anderson's eyes narrowed. "Still carrying a torch for the deputy. I should have lit the match as soon as I had you."

"I-is he still ... alive?" *Please, let him be alive.*

Anderson snorted. "For now. I knew I wouldn't get your cooperation if you knew for sure Wilburn was dead. Last I checked, he's in that cabin flat on his back like a bloated fish."

Ollie closed her eyes. Titus still lived.

"Now we get married." Anderson wrapped his hand around her biceps with a vice grip.

She had to stall and give someone a chance to find her. "B-but who will marry us? Judge Cavanaugh would never, the preacher neither."

"See, that's just it, Olivia." He cut the rope tying her hands to her feet and pulled her out of the hollow into the snowy forest. It would be quiet, and peaceful, beautiful at any other moment. "We will have our own ceremony. You and me. We don't need them. You'll be my wife as soon as I get you home."

Panic gripped her. "No."

His slap came out of nowhere, and her body jerked with the impact.

"If you ever use that word again with me, you will feel much worse."

A whimper slipped out. Is this what Seth dealt with every day? The poor boy! His only aim was to please. "Did you make Seth leave the gifts?"

Anderson barked a laugh. "The kid was so gullible, just like his mother. Then she went and got a backbone when I wanted to get rid of Seth, so I had to get rid of her."

Bile rose in Ollie's throat. Did *get rid of* mean what she thought it meant?

Anderson shoved his face within inches of hers. "And if you don't follow exactly what I say, I will get rid of you. Or maybe I will get rid of that deputy of yours and make you watch."

A gust blew snow into her face, and like the cold slap it was, she realized she had only one choice. To acquiesce, to follow along would be a living death, a constant fear, and likely get Titus killed along the way. But fighting back? It might cost her life, even Titus's life … unless they succeeded.

She raised her chin. "I won't marry you until I am sure Titus is safe, and I have assurances he will stay safe."

A growl rumbled low in Anderson's throat.

Ollie ignored it, and the fear it threatened to stoke. "Then we do this the right way. We get the preacher and have the ceremony in a church." It was the only way she could think of buying time.

Anderson pulled out a knife, and she flinched away. Then he cut her ropes and hauled her into his arms. "I knew you'd see it my way. I knew you wanted to marry me."

And then he began to sway. It took her a moment to realize he was dancing. With her. In the snow. She squeezed her eyes shut as revulsion shot shivers down her cold body. "I will never love someone who would force me into marriage, who uses his fists to get his way."

Anderson pushed her to the ground. The cold snow swallowed her. With no coat, her clothing dampened instantly. Quicker than her mind could follow, he flipped her face into the snow and trussed her up again. Then he dragged her into the snow cave and tossed the pelts on her.

"I'd leave you to freeze to death, but I want you to suffer first. You will see your lord, and I will make him leap. Then he will die, and you will be mine."

Titus was going to lose his mind.

He couldn't walk, so he couldn't pace. He couldn't escape the cabin, either. The blizzard had shredded the last of his self-control. Only Osborn's calm had kept him from diving out into the snow when Osborn had returned without sign of her. Peace of God wasn't what he felt.

But now the snow had stopped. Osborn had left an hour ago to check on his animals and care for Titus's horse, leaving him alone in the cabin with nothing but his swirling thoughts.

Had Casper found Seth? Had they been caught in the blizzard? And what would he say to Eira Mae if Casper had been injured in the storm? He wouldn't know until Osborn returned. After the man finished morning chores, he would return to town to organize a search party.

Titus leaned his head against the back of the rocker. He couldn't do a dratted thing but sit here waiting and praying and begging.

Grabbing his walking stick, he bit back the pain throbbing in his lower back and hobbled to the bookshelf. He needed to hear Ollie's voice in his head and the best way would be to read a book she'd read to him. He scanned the shelves, slowing when he came to Casper's collection by Charles Dickens. He'd enjoyed Ollie's reading of *A Christmas Carol*. How had it begun? *Marley was dead to begin with.* He plucked it from the shelf and returned to the rocker.

He stumbled when he came to the place where Nephew Fred joyously greeted Ebenezer Scrooge.

"Christmas a humbug, uncle!" said Scrooge's nephew. "You don't mean that, I am sure?"

"I do," said Scrooge. "Merry Christmas! What right have you to be merry? What reason have you to be merry? You're poor enough."

"Come, then," returned the nephew gaily. "What right have you to be dismal?

What right did Titus have to be merry? He could hardly walk, his future looked bleak. Worst of all, he couldn't rescue his love. Yet, he hated that he sounded like Scrooge. He hated that his spirit echoed the words of the cross old man.

"What else can I be … when I live in such a world of fools as this? Merry Christmas! Out upon merry Christmas! What's Christmas time to you but a time for paying bills without money; a time for finding yourself a year older, but not an hour richer; a time for balancing your books and having every item in 'em through a round dozen of months presented dead against you?"

Like a parched man, Titus drank in Nephew Fred's insistence on celebration, his good humor despite

Scrooge's humbug replies. Like Ollie. So much like Ollie. Titus's heart cracked. He would trade a hale and healthy body if it meant having her beside him the rest of his days.

The spirit of Marley's ghost had just appeared to Scrooge when Titus heard footsteps crunching the snow outside. The book jumped in his hands. *Ghost story, indeed.* It was too early for Osborn to have returned with Casper, and both would call out. That meant Ollie's abductor had returned.

Titus set the book, pages splayed, spine up, on the table beside the lantern, which he blew out. Then he slipped the knife he'd kept since peeling potatoes into the sheath tucked within his boot and unbuckled his holster. By the time he used the walking stick to push to his feet, a masked man stood in the open door, a pistol aimed at Titus.

"What bargain can we make?" Titus limped forward. "You alone?"

Titus nodded and the man pulled down his mask. Not Seth. Titus squinted, trying to place him. He looked familiar. "Adam Anderson." Clean-shaven and not smelling like a still.

Anderson grunted. "Leave your coat and get walking. One wrong move and Olivia's life is in your hands."

Titus shuffled into the snow. His back screamed at each step, but Anderson's laugh had him fighting through. For Ollie, he could do this. He had to. She couldn't sacrifice a lifetime married to Anderson for Titus. Even as the pain worsened with each stumbling step, as his arms grew weaker with hauling himself through the snow with his walking stick, his resolve only hardened to steel. This might cost him his legs, which would cost him his job. There wasn't even a guarantee he would make it away from Anderson alive. However, for Ollie, it was worth it.

His only hope was the message he'd left behind. Osborn would return with Casper. Casper would have talked to Seth. They would see the book left open, the holster left behind, and know Titus had given himself up. Behind him, Anderson attempted to hide their path by smoothing the snow, but Titus' walking stick dug deep. His feet waded through. His occasional stumble splashed snow outside their path. Osborn and Casper were both expert trackers. They'd find him, dead or alive, which meant, if he could stall long enough, they would find Ollie, too.

CHAPTER THIRTEEN

Deeper into the woods they traveled, and except for Titus's dragging steps, he began to doubt whether even Osborn could find them or whether Ollie could find her way back out. He wouldn't, he knew that. Not to mention, daylight would only last a few more hours, and after that ... darkness.

When they finally reached the snow hollow where Anderson had kept Ollie, Titus's body shook with pain and weariness. Sweat chilled him. Each ragged breath knifed through him like an icy blade. But the relief at seeing Ollie's eyes widen when Anderson pulled her from the hollow gave him the strength to prepare to fight for her freedom.

"Titus," Ollie whispered. Anderson had her by the biceps, her hands bound behind her, her ankles roped together. Anderson pushed her to the ground, then gave him a shove and he landed beside Ollie with a cry of pain.

"Whining isn't going to win you any favors," Anderson grunted.

"I don't need favors." Titus leaned against Ollie. He needed her to be free.

"Can't you see he's in pain?" Ollie glared at Anderson.

Anderson jabbed a gloved finger at her. "When the sun goes down, you are coming with me. He is staying here. So say your goodbyes now, and if you so much as give a hint of protest, I will shoot him in front of you instead of leaving him for the animals to find."

As soon as Anderson disappeared into the woods, Titus pressed his head against Ollie's. "We're going to get out of this." If only he could remember his plan. His ears buzzed, his thoughts swam.

"I know." Ollie sounded as if she had no doubt, which encouraged him. Behind her back, she worked the rope around her raw wrists. "I don't know how, but together, we will. I won't leave you here."

"You have to." That was the plan. "I can't go any farther, but I can distract Anderson long enough for you to get away, get help. Please, Ollie."

She cocked her head, studying him, reading him, and it made him look away. She nudged his shoulder. "You know I liked you before you became a deputy."

Pain again encroached on his ability to think. "What does it have to do with this?"

"Even if you can't walk, even if you can't be a deputy, I still love you."

He stared at her, absorbing her words. They watered the seed that had been planted while reading Dickens's tale.

"Remember, you told me you don't want to be sheriff? That you like being the second in command because you prefer helping widows and rescuing cats from trees. Neighborly kinds of things, but not necessarily police keeping. Do you still feel that way?"

Titus nodded, surety taking root.

"Good. Because even without all those things, you are more than enough for me." She leaned close and kissed his cheek.

"Isn't that sweet?" Anderson strode into the tiny clearing, tapping a cattle prod against his palm. "Let's see how well Mr. Deputy can march."

"Leave him alone." Ollie rose up on her knees.

Anderson aimed the cattle prod at her. "Best learn silence now, my love."

"Stop." Titus hauled himself to his feet using his walking stick. "Do what you want to me, but let her go."

Anderson chuckled. "This is too good. The two of you continually trying to defend the other. You make it so easy, and here I thought this would be difficult. Threaten one, and the other does exactly what I want. And I want the girl."

Titus planted his feet and coiled his muscles, knowing he would have one shot at this. If he survived the next few moments, the action he was about to take could land him unable to walk for the rest of his life. He braced himself for the pain and sprung.

"Titus, no!" Ollie screamed as Titus launched himself at Mr. Anderson.

Anderson's shocked expression matched her own surprise and gave Titus the edge he needed to knock Anderson to the ground. The cattle prod flew from Anderson's hands as the men rolled in the snow.

Numb through and through and still bound, she was helpless to do anything but watch. Anderson landed a punch and managed to land on top of Titus. Titus didn't try to buck him off, and he didn't move. Had Anderson rendered him unconscious? Ollie froze at the malicious smile that spread across Anderson's face.

With sudden speed, Titus flipped Anderson and pinned his walking stick against the man's neck. Anderson kicked and flailed, and Titus's arms gave out. He sprawled over Anderson's face, keeping the stick in place, until Anderson slowly stopped moving.

"Is he ..." Ollie stared.

Titus shook his head and rolled into the snow. "Unconscious."

Ollie shuffled her knees to Titus's side. "Are you okay?"

"Knife in my boot."

It took longer than she liked for her to maneuver her bound hands and frozen fingers to capture the knife. Titus took it from her and cut the ropes.

"Tie his legs." Titus closed his eyes. "Arms, too."

Ollie obeyed, then scrambled back to him. "Now what?"

But Titus had lost consciousness.

Think, Ollie. She forced herself not to panic, not to allow fear to muddle her. She had to get help, but she couldn't leave. She glanced back at the hollow, then at Anderson, and back to Titus. She wasn't strong enough to move either man, but she could cover them with the pelts.

Slipping and sliding over numb feet, she raced the oncoming darkness. Afraid Anderson would wake while she was gone, she dragged a large, dead branch over to him, pushed him onto his side, and tied it to his back with the rope he had left in the hollow. Then, after double-checking her knots and kissing Titus on the forehead, she followed their tracks back toward home.

Not far from her destination, she heard her and Titus's names echoing through the trees. Multiple male voices. She recognized Grandfather among them and shouted back.

Relief hit hard as he raced toward her faster than she'd ever seen him move. She collapsed into his embrace, tears cascading down her cheeks.

"Titus?" Casper demanded.

Ollie sniffed and pulled away from Grandfather to answer, only then seeing the number of rescuers who had come to their aid. She recognized all but two, a young man and an old one.

"Titus?" Grandfather nudged her.

"That way." Ollie pointed back to where she'd come from. "Adam Anderson is tied up next to him. He's the one who kidnapped us."

"Lundgren, with me." Casper pointed to the younger man she hadn't recognized, then to the older one. "O'Connor, stay with Ollie and Osborn, would you?"

The older man, O'Connor, gave a single nod, though his bushy gray eyebrow twitched and his full gray mustache bobbed.

"Casper will see to Titus." Grandfather urged her toward Casper's cabin, which was closer than his. "Meet Detective Michael O'Connor. Apparently, you weren't the only female in trouble this weekend. His nephew was seriously injured. Took me a time of it finding Casper and Lundgren because of it."

"Will your nephew be okay?" Ollie asked the detective.

"I think we got to him in time." He had a gravelly voice. "Trouble up at Aleric Lumber Camp."

She knew the name, since lumbermen occasionally came to town. Though only Mrs. Nelson, the lumber camp cook, ever visited the library these days. She liked the older lady and always extended the customary book loan period so she could take a book with her back to camp.

Back at the cabin, Grandfather insisted she change into warm clothes and heated water to soak her feet and hands. Detective O'Connor told her tales from his hometown, a place called Crow's Nest. He told fine ones about his fisherman nephew and the stranger who won his heart, about a cowboy who fell in love with an archaeologist, and a particularly annoying man whom the detective was determined to arrest if he could just gather enough evidence. It kept the worry from consuming her while she waited for Casper to return with Titus.

But Casper didn't. Instead, one of the searchers from town delivered a message that they'd taken Titus and Anderson straight back to town. Ollie insisted on leaving at once, and neither Grandfather nor O'Connor argued with her.

That night, she sat beside Titus's bed above the sheriff's office, her grandfather dozing nearby on a cot Casper had provided. Titus woke off and on, but the doctor had provided strong pain medicine that kept him incoherent. The doctor explained that the bruising and swelling of his lower back were most concerning, and they needed to keep him immobile as much as possible, or he might never walk again.

CHAPTER FOURTEEN

Thursday, December 25
1st Day of Christmas

"You think Ollie will like it?" Titus tested out his new chair in the open space between his desk and Casper's. Osborn and O'Connor had helped him fashion it out of old wheels and a broken high back chair. While he could walk with the support of a walking stick, it was slow going. His new chair would allow him to move about town more easily.

Casper folded his arms and laughed. "I think every kid in town is going to want a ride."

Titus stopped in the middle of the room and removed the gloves that protected his palms. "You sure about this?"

Casper pulled his desk chair around and sat with his arms across the back. "You and Ollie make superb county employees. Between you both, you'll manage the library and all the paperwork I can't stomach here at the jailhouse. I'm sure my uncle's secretary would be happy to share if you're feeling bored."

"I hate paperwork." Titus rubbed his thighs. There was a chance walking would become easier as he regained his strength, but the doctor warned another injury, even age, could reverse his progress. "I want to be useful."

"Useful isn't enough, Titus." Casper pinned him with that intense stare. "How about vital? I'm not offering you this position just to placate you. The last few days showed me we need a permanent person stationed at the jailhouse—someone who lives here and can operate any calls that come in. Osborn couldn't find me or Lundgren because we were with O'Connor. If we have one person who knows where everyone is and can help manage priorities, it will mean a safer town."

The words sank in, and Titus believed them. They echoed what Ollie told him every day.

"Not to mention, now you'll have more time—and the wheels—to help all the widows who've been clamoring for a real hero to help them."

Titus mirrored Casper's grin. "Getting carried into town on a stretcher has that effect."

The jailhouse door opened. "Well, well, well. What is this?" Ollie hiked her bag of books higher on her shoulder.

"My surprise, Mrs. Wilburn." Titus didn't waste time putting on the gloves and wheeled about the room, stopping directly in front of his bride of one day. "What do you think?"

"It's marvelous!" Ollie's eyes shone like bright stars. "Now I know why you sent me to the library. You didn't really want me to pick up more books to read to you."

"Oh, but I did." Titus tugged her onto his lap. "I never tire of your reading to me, and since I left *A*

Christmas Carol unfinished at Casper's cabin, that is my first request."

"And that is my cue." Casper shrugged on his coat and gathered a box he'd brought with him this morning. "Eira Mae is already at my aunt and uncle's with her whole family. Are you sure you both don't want to join us for Christmas dinner? Lundgren is spending it with his mother and siblings."

They both shook their heads. Titus had no interest in sharing Ollie with anyone.

"I figured." Casper chuckled, then held out the box. "Oh, before I leave. Seth asked if he could give you both a wedding gift. He had no idea what his father was doing, I have no doubts about that. The man used his son and won't be able to hurt him again."

"What will happen to Seth?" Ollie asked. She would not reach for the box.

"Mrs. Holland has decided to take him in. She'll pay him in room and board for help around the Inn. It sounds like O'Connor's group will be in town for a while. They don't want to leave until Meri's baby is born if they can help it. And O'Connor will fill in for me so I can help Eira Mae until the baby arrives." Casper attempted to hide a giddy grin behind his fist. "Doc said he expects the baby at the end of January."

"Enjoy the time with your family, Cas." Titus took the box from him. "You deserve it."

"So do you." Casper slapped his shoulder. "Merry Christmas, Mr. and Mrs. Wilburn."

Ollie rested her head on Titus's shoulder as the jailhouse door closed. Living in a jail. Who would have guessed? But as long as she was with Titus, she could live anywhere.

"Shall we open this?" Titus shook the white box.

"I suppose so." Ollie lifted the lid with clammy hands. Inside lay twelve carefully carved toy drummers. But what drew her attention was the note. She lifted it out and read:

"Ollie and Titus, I am sorry my gift scared you and that my dad hurt you. That was wrong. I heard a wedding is supposed to have a wedding march. These drummers can't really drum, but you can pretend. I am staying with Mrs. Holland now. She's a lot nicer than my dad. Merry Christmas. Seth."

A tear dripped down Ollie's cheek and splashed on the paper. "He's such a sweet boy."

"Not a boy." Titus lifted a drummer. "He's a man and does fantastic handiwork. Perhaps I can apprentice him. I can't do all the work I used to, but he might be interested. He deserves to be treated with respect."

Ollie swiped at a second tear. "You're a good man, Titus Wilburn. A hero. My hero."

"An unlikely one." Titus wheeled them closer to the desk to set down the box with its drummers and letter. "But you've made me feel like a hero because of how you see me. If I can do that for Seth, I want to try."

Ollie kissed him squarely on the cheek. "I have a casserole to set in the oven so we have something to eat. Does that chair stay down here or come along to our quarters?"

"Hand me my walking stick, darling." Titus grinned at her and tapped the bag that still hung from her shoulder. "You have my book in there?"

Ollie slid from his lap. "Books by Charles Dickens and Beatrix Potter."

"Perfect." Titus pushed himself from the chair.

He'd improved remarkably since that day in the woods, but would probably never walk with ease again. He'd sacrificed his future for her. But as she continually reminded him that she loved him whether he could run or never walk again; he reminded her that he would give his life for hers.

Ollie supposed that was the essence of love: giving everything to one another, not just on this first day of Christmas, but every day. As was said of Scrooge, may it be said of them, that they knew how to keep Christmas well every day of the year.

Titus rested his free arm over her shoulders, and she wrapped her arm around his waist. Supporting one another, loving one another. They climbed the stairs. Slow, but sure. Together.

"And so, as Tiny Tim observed …" The words slipped out as they reached their rooms above the jailhouse.

Titus cupped her cheek. "God bless us, everyone."

Then he nodded toward the mistletoe that hadn't been above the door when he'd sent her to get the books that morning—and winked.

The Christmas Cabin Novella series continues in
July 2026 with Gideon Lundgren's story:
The Robbers and the Witness

#

Love Christmas Novellas?
Read on for an excerpt from
Escape with the Prodigal

ESCAPE WITH THE PRODIGAL

Monday, December 21, 1931
Eastern Minnesota

A gust of snowy air propelled Evangeline Whitaker through the train station door. The warmth of the potbelly stove in the center of the room enveloped her in a welcoming hug, a pleasant sensation after the painful goodbye she had just finished with her brother.

The scent of pine from the Christmas wreath beside the door encouraged her to inhale deeply, then let out her breath slowly. Her quiet steps emptied in the empty station as she walked across the small room, and she settled her carpetbag on the wooden bench close to the stove before seating herself next to it. With the train to Chicago gone, her brother aboard, the bustle of the station had ebbed. She was now, for all intents and purposes, alone.

Until her brother's best friend arrived, of course.

Her stomach fluttered at the thought. She hadn't seen Gideon Lundgren in nearly a decade, though he and Evan kept up through regular correspondence. Gideon wouldn't be the boy she remembered—Evangeline knew that. Still, she hoped he still had that underlying kindness that offset Evan's annoying perfectionism. Especially since she had to spend the Christmas holiday with the family of Gideon's boss. Would Gideon be there too?

The clock on the wall ticked loudly. Gideon's train had been due half an hour ago, but apparently there was snow on the tracks and his train had been delayed. It did not bode well for the return trip, back to the town where he now worked as a deputy.

Lord, my wish is to not spend Christmas in the station all alone.

A tall, rail-thin man entered the train station, a knapsack slung over his bony shoulder. He was wiry, his tattered old coat hanging from him. He looked almost hollow. A knit cap pulled low over his eyes, he gave Evangeline a nod as he passed her. She tracked his movements as he walked across the dim space toward the stationmaster's ticketing counter.

He purchased a ticket, then wandered back toward Evangeline. She couldn't help but watch him. Was it his ghost-like quality? She could almost picture him going up in a cloud of snow, disappearing like smoke from the stove.

The man approached, glanced over at the ticket master, then spoke to her, his voice hesitant and quiet. "I need to see the privy. Can you ... can you watch after my bag?"

"Sure," Evangeline said with a shrug. Why not? There was no harm in someone setting their bag next to her.

She wasn't about to rummage through it, and she would be here until Gideon's train pulled in.

The man gave a nod and set the bulky knapsack beside her, shifting her carpetbag out of the way. "Thank you, miss."

She watched him walk out the rear of the building where the outdoor privies were located. She could hear her brother's voice in her head, scolding her for speaking to a strange man. If Evan were here, she would comment on how no harm would come from simply watching a bag beside her.

Continue reading in
The Robber and the Witness
For details, visit:
daniellegrandinetti.com/the-robber-and-the-witness

FROM THE AUTHOR

Dear Reader,

Thank you for reading Titus and Ollie's story. I hope you enjoyed reading their friends-to-more romance. If you haven't read the story of Titus' boss, Casper, and Eira Mae's romance, you can find it in *The Baby and the Guardian*: daniellegrandinetti.com/the-baby-and-the-guardian.

Special thanks to my editors Ann Elizabeth Fryer, Sarah Hinkle, and my proofreaders for making this story shine. And a great big thank you to my husband and boys for giving me the time to turn these thoughts into a story for you. I love writing Christmas novellas and Christmas music, so it's been such fun to pair the two in this story. If you've enjoyed *The Neighbor and the Gifts*, I'd be most grateful if you'd take a moment to leave an honest review.

Follow the Christmas Cabin series page on my website to discover Gideon's story and how the Christmas Cabin brings love to his life. And, don't miss Sheriff Yarwood's appearance in *Escape with the Prodigal*, book three (and stand-alone Christmas novella) of my historical romance series Harbored in Crow's Nest. A holiday romance filled with danger, redemption, and sacrifice: daniellegrandinetti.com/escape-with-the-prodigal.

I hope you enjoyed *The Neighbor and the Gifts* and I'd be honored if you would leave an honest review on your preferred retail site. As always, I'd love to keep in touch. Visit my website at daniellegrandinetti.com for where to follow me, and be sure to sign up for my weekly newsletter at daniellegrandinetti.com/fsn for all the bookish news.

Thank you for joining me for Titus and Ollie's Christmas adventure!

Happy reading!

Danielle Grandinetti

HISTORICAL NOTES

From what I've seen, when *The Twelve Days of Christmas* is the basis of a story, the hero or heroine is the one delivering the gifts in various ways (I especially love Karen Witemeyer's take in *My True Love Gave to Me*). The history of the poem and song are difficult to trace. According to the Smithsonian Magazine, the poem was originally published in *Mirth Without Mischief* in 1780, but has been around much longer.

Here is a list of the twelve gifts mentioned in the poem:

Twelve drummers drumming

Eleven pipers piping

Ten lords a-leaping

Nine ladies dancing

Eight maids a-milking

Seven swans a-swimming

Six geese a-laying

Five golden rings

Four calling birds

Three French hens

Two turtle doves

A partridge in a pear tree

I got to thinking ... what if the bad guy in a suspense story—a stalker—was the one giving the gifts? Only, the term *stalker* wasn't used in this sense until the late 1900s. Thus commenced the research into the history of stalking. Britannica provided the most succinct explanation into what we term today as "stalking." During the early 1900s and before, it had a psychiatric term: Erotomania. It's "the delusion of being loved by someone, often a prominent or even famous person." Sounds like stalking right? Only, back then, erotomaniacs tended to be female as opposed to today when stalkers are often male. However, at the end of the day, an *erotomaniac* according to Etymology online is "one driven mad by passionate love." A perfect opportunity to run with my story idea.

A few other interesting historical notes ...

Partridges are not native to Wisconsin. Pheasant is, which is why I used that bird in the story.

The Leghorn chicken originates from a region in Northern Italy and arrived in America in the mid-1800's.

And the wheelchair Titus constructed is based on the one FDR made himself, which you can learn more about on the National Park Service's blog.

JOIN MY FIRESIDE NEWS

Grab a spot on my virtual hearth to receive my weekly email, and as a thank you you'll receive a digital copy of my novelette *Fire and Water*. Subscribe at daniellegrandinetti.com/fsn

CHRISTMAS CABIN SERIES

One cabin in the Northwoods ... a decade of Christmas miracles.

daniellegrandinetti.com/christmas-cabin-series

The Sheriff and the Outlaw

CHRISTMAS CABIN, PREQUEL

Discover the beginning of the Christmas Cabin series

in this Christmas suspense short story.

The Baby and the Guardian

Christmas Cabin, #1
**A baby in danger, a man in turmoil,
and a woman determined to save them both.**

The Neighbor and the Gifts

Christmas Cabin, #2
**Twelve days. Twelve gifts.
One unlikely hero.**

The Robber and the Witness

Christmas Cabin, #3
**A simple favor, a best friend's promise,
and the end of the line.
Releasing July 2026**

HARBORED IN CROW'S NEST

Welcome to Crow's Nest,
where danger and romance meet at the water's edge.
danillegrandinetti.com/harbored-in-crows-nest

Confessions to a Stranger

Harbored in Crow's Nest, #1

She's lost her future. He's sacrificed his.
Now they have a chance to reclaim it—together.

Refuge for the Archaeologist

Harbored in Crow's Nest, #2

*Will uncovering the truth set them free
or destroy what they hold most dear?*

Escape with the Prodigal

Harbored in Crow's Nest, #3

*Only a Christmas miracle will save
an unwed mother and the lumberjack protecting her.*

Relying on the Enemy

Harbored in Crow's Nest, #4

*She's protecting her children.
He's redeeming his past.*

Sheltered by the Doctor

Harbored in Crow's Nest, #5

*A fake relationship might keep her safe,
but will it break their hearts?*

Investigation of a Journalist

HARBORED IN CROW'S NEST, #6

A second chance to set the record straight,
and rekindle a lost love.

DI STASIO GIORNALISTE AGENCY

La Verità con Integrità. Truth with Integrity.
The Legacy of a (Girl) Stunt Reporter.
daniellegrandinetti.com/di-stasio-giornaliste-agency

Undercover Wish

DI STASIO GIORNALISTE AGENCY, #0

DANIELLE GRANDINETTI

Alessandra Di Stasio
Chicago World's Fair: World's Columbian Exposition

Eyewitness Sketch

DI STASIO GIORNALISTE AGENCY, #1
Gabriella Salatino
Prohibition

Sabotage Games

DI STASIO GIORNALISTE AGENCY, #2
Emma Hancock
Summer & Winter Olympics: Lake Placid & L.A.

Shrouded Trail

DI STASIO GIORNALISTE AGENCY, #3
Lena Carney
Presidential Election

Fraudulent Progress

DI STASIO GIORNALISTE AGENCY, #4

OUR HOUSE NOVELLAS

As the world marches toward what will become WWII, visit Our House as we join the resistance.

The Italian Musician's Sanctuary
Romance, history and intrigue at Our House on Sycamore Street.

Hunted by one man, can she open her heart to another?
Eden Cove, England, 1931—Margherita Vicienzo flees Italy pursued by her former fiancé, a

member of Mussolini's Blackshirt. Smuggled illegally into England, Margherita is a foreigner at the mercy of strangers. Her limp from an improperly healed broken leg means she has nothing to offer the Ferryman family, who offer her sanctuary, and nothing to appease their son who resents her presence.

Luke Ferryman needs a wife. He wants to marry for love, but carries the weight of his family's generations-old expectations on his shoulders. Though he inherited the role of both baker and ferryman, he knows he can't fulfill both needs once his aging grandparents retire. A wife would help, but not an illegal one like the refugee his matchmaking grandmother is harboring.

As opposite as night and day, Luke and Margherita forge a tentative friendship that grows despite the constant threat of Margherita's discovery. But when strangers appear in the close-knit seaside town, threatening Luke's livelihood and Margherita's safety, the choice between justice and mercy becomes harder. And sacrifice proves the only answer.

The Recluse's Vindication
Rumors, Monsters, and Second Chances
at Our House on Heather Wynd

The Loch Ness Monster isn't the only recluse seeking a Scottish haven.

Bieldfell, Scotland, 1933—Falsely accused of murder sixteen years ago, American cowboy Benjamin Ford has chosen to hide out in the Scottish Highlands. Reclusive and not afraid to die, he rescues children out of an increasingly dangerous Germany. When his childhood best friend appears at his door, he's not the boy she remembers.

Eleanor Finch's life ended sixteen years ago. In one horrible day, she lost her dreams, her reputation, and her heart. However, she never gives up the hope of finding her friend, so when she learns of Ben's whereabouts, she leaves all that is familiar to convince him to return home.

But Eleanor isn't the only person searching for Ben. Hunters follow her trail. The thin veil of gossip and rumor may be their only chance of a future ... unless the Loch Ness Monster is real after all.

DANIELLE GRANDINETTI

daniellegrandinetti.com/our-house

FAIRYTALE RETELLINGS

HEART OF BEAUTY

stand-alone origin novella

Discover the origin of Crooked Tooth Ranch in this 1870s western retelling of Beauty and the Beast.

daniellegrandinetti.com/heart-of-beauty

His Boss's Little Sister

stand-alone novella in the Apron Strings
Tea Tale multi-author series

A touch of fairy tale, a spoonful of history, and a teacup of hope ... a 1930s historical romance retelling of Hansel and Gretel.

daniellegrandinetti.com/his-bosss-little-sis
ter

Undercover Wish

stand-alone novella, part of the Di Stasio
Giornaliste Agency series

A Di Stasio Giornaliste Agency origin story and a retelling of Aladdin and the Magic Lamp.

daniellegrandinetti.com/heart-of-beauty

UNEXPECTED PROTECTORS

Visit small-town Wisconsin during the Dairy Strikes of the Great Depression in these three historical romances.

For details, visit:

daniellegrandinetti.com/unexpected-protectors

To Stand in the Breach

Strike to the Heart, #1

She came to America to escape a workhouse prison, but will the cost of freedom be too high a price to pay?

A Strike to the Heart

STRIKE TO THE HEART, #2
She's fiercely independent.
He's determined to protect her.

As Silent as the Night

STRIKE TO THE HEART, #3
He can procure anything, except his heart's deepest wish.
She might hold the key, if she's not discovered first.

ABOUT THE AUTHOR

Danielle Grandinetti is an award-winning author of 1930s historical romance, where mystery and suspense intertwine with hope. Her work has received recognition including a Distinguished Faith in Writing Award, two National Excellence in Storytelling Awards, and finalist honors in the FHLCW Reader's Choice, Selah, and Daphne du Maurier contests.

A second-generation Italian-American rooted in Midwest traditions, Danielle draws inspiration from tea, books, and the creative beauty of nature. Holding a master's in communication and culture, and driven by a lifelong love of stories, she crafts tales that celebrate resilience, diversity, and belonging. Danielle lives along Wisconsin's Lake Michigan shoreline with her husband and two sons. Find her online at daniellegrandinetti.com.